PIPER TUMBLED BACKWA[...]
WITHOUT WARNING. SWIFTLY, C. K. MOVED [...]
OF THE LIVING ROOM, PUTTING DISTANCE BETWEEN
HERSELF AND THE CHARMED ONES.

"Her face," Phoebe whispered urgently. "Look at her face. I don't think that happened last time. Malvolio's possession of her must be almost total."

Piper nodded as Paige helped her get to her feet. "No two ways about it. He's definitely getting stronger."

C. K. looked around the room, her eyes glittering wildly.

"I require a vehicle," she said. "You will provide one."

"Okay," Phoebe said, as she carefully got up. "No problem. Mind if we come along for the ride?"

C. K. smiled. "Foolish witches," she said. "You think that you can stop me? I am stronger than you can possibly imagine. No power on this earth can prevent what I am about to unleash."

"I'll take that as a yes," Phoebe said. She headed for the front hall. Yanking her keys from her purse, she lobbed them across the room toward C. K. "You drive."

BETWEEN WORLDS

Charmed®

Published by Simon & Schuster

Charmed ®

BETWEEN WORLDS

An original novel by

Bobbi J. G. Weiss and Jacklyn Wilson

Based on the hit TV series created by

Constance M. Burge

SIMON SPOTLIGHT ENTERTAINMENT

New York   London   Toronto   Sydney

First Simon Pulse edition September 2003
First Simon Spotlight Entertainment edition May 2004

S|S|E

SIMON SPOTLIGHT ENTERTAINMENT
An imprint of Simon & Schuster
Children's Publishing Division
1230 Avenue of the Americas
New York, NY 10020

SIMON SPOTLIGHT ENTERTAINMENT and related logo are
trademarks of Simon & Schuster, Inc.
The colophon is a trademark of Simon & Schuster.

The text of this book was set in Palatino.

Printed in the United States of America

10 9 8 7 6 5 4

Library of Congress Control Number 2003105592

ISBN 0-689-85792-6

One

The apartment was small and organized within an inch of its life.

The couch was a fifties reproduction, straight-backed, stiff-armed. A row of square chenille pillows marched along its length. All the same size and color, each one was an equal distance from the ones on either side. A glass-topped coffee table, a large leather-bound book precisely in its center, sat two and one half feet in front of the couch.

Plants were made of silk. Nothing here would be allowed to wither, allowed to die. Bookshelves, their contents as precisely arranged as in a library, lined the living room walls.

In the bathroom, not a faucet dripped. In the bedroom, the bed was made with military precision, so tight and smooth that a quarter bounced off its surface would have traveled halfway to the ceiling before coming back down. In the kitchen, not a glass sat on the counter, not a fork remained unwashed.

Lights blazed brightly in every room, illuminating the order, even though it was the middle of the night. In the entire apartment, not a thing was out of place.

Except for one: its occupant.

The woman was young, mid-twenties tops. Dressed in a pair of soft and ancient jeans, scuffed sneakers, and a sweatshirt dotted by food spots, she looked as if she hadn't changed her clothes or showered in days. Her soft blond hair was wild around her head, as if she'd combed her fingers through it millions of times. Her fingernails were bitten down to the quick.

And her eyes . . .

Her eyes were enormous and bloodshot, fixed on the leather book resting in the very center of her coffee table. The same book she'd thrown into the downstairs dumpster that very morning, just as she'd done the day before. And the day before that. Every single day for almost a week now. Ever since she'd come home from the magic store to find the book in her shoulder bag. That much, she was sure she remembered clearly.

What she couldn't remember was putting it there herself.

I never should have gone to that store in the first place. If I hadn't, none of this wouldn't have happened. I was weak, and this is what I get, she thought. *If Jace were here, he'd—*

With a sound of dismay, the young woman pressed one hand against her quivering mouth. She would not cry. Not now. Not after all this time. Not when she'd made it almost an entire year without giving in to her grief.

Because Jace Fraser, her fiancé, wasn't here. That was the whole problem.

But he could be. If only . . .

"No!" the young woman cried aloud. She bolted up from the dining chair on which she'd been sitting, its ladder back pressed against her front door. She'd been there all day, determined that nothing would get into her apartment without her knowledge.

But the book had still come back. Somehow.

"I won't take that way!" she proclaimed as she paced wildly around the room, long beyond finding it strange that she was talking to herself. She'd been doing that for days as well. Ever since she'd opened her shoulder bag to find the book nestled down inside it like a snake curled inside a stump.

An analogy that was only fitting, as there was a serpent embossed on its thick leather cover.

Ever since then, it was as if some devil's advocate had come to life inside her head, urging her to take actions she couldn't consider. To explore avenues she didn't even know how to explore. She'd tried to resist. She'd been trying, alone in her apartment, for nearly a week now. She'd called in sick for work, which she never did. Afraid to let anyone see her, see the usually precise, controlled C. K. Piers acting like she belonged on a soap opera set in the crisis intervention unit of a psych ward.

But she was growing weaker. She could feel it. Because there was something she wanted, so very, very much.

"I won't take that path. I won't! Do you hear me?" she shouted. Maybe if she said it loudly enough, often enough, she could continue to convince herself.

The path the voice was urging upon her ran counter to everything C. K. believed in. Everything she understood and accepted. About the world. About herself. She didn't know why she'd been born with the power to do things other people couldn't. She didn't want an explanation. Just as she'd never really wanted the power, itself.

Or so she'd always told herself.

Why are you being so stubborn about this? the voice that had been tormenting her all week spoke up now. *You have the power, why not use it? You can't go on keeping what you feel bottled up inside. That's not healthy. If you'd ever actually consent to see a therapist, I'm sure he'd tell you so.*

"She," C. K. automatically answered out loud. Go to see a male therapist. As if. No longer even aware that she was doing it, C. K. ran her fingers through her filthy hair as if the action would pull the voice right out of her head.

Go away! Why won't you go away?

"Jace," she sobbed.

But Jace wants you to do this, don't you see? the voice spoke up once more. *He wants to be with you. Why don't you stop struggling and help him? Your refusal is only hurting him. Is that what you want? If so, you didn't love him very much.*

"That's not true!" C. K. cried. "I did love Jace. I mean, I *do* love him. More than anything in the world. That didn't stop just because he's . . ."

Dead. Brutally, the voice inside her head cut her off. *Jace is dead, C. K. He died a year ago. But you won't let him rest, you're in so much denial. You won't help him. You won't even help yourself. You're pathetic. What Jace ever saw in you, I'll never know.*

Tears streamed down C. K.'s cheeks to dampen the top of her sweatshirt. She made no attempt to stop them.

"Jace and I were soul mates," she whispered. "He understood me. He's the only one who ever did. We were perfect for each other."

Then prove it, the voice whispered, soothing, comforting, now. *Perform the spell. You have everything you need. It won't take long. Then you and Jace can be together again. Isn't that what you want? Using your power to put an end to pain isn't wrong, C. K. On the contrary, that's what it's for.*

C. K.'s shoulders sagged and she stopped pacing. *Why on earth am I putting up such a fight?* she wondered. Surely, the voice was right. Using her power to put an end to pain had to be considered a good thing, not a bad one. Particularly if it could end Jace's pain as well as her own.

And she *did* want Jace back. More than that, she *needed* him. Jace had been the only one who'd ever loved her just as she was. In response, she'd built her whole world around him.

C. K.'s coworkers might marvel at how well she'd coped during the past year, ever since Jace had been killed in a hit-and-run auto accident, but that was only because C.K.'d never let them see how she felt inside. Empty. Alone. The truth was, C. K. was lost without Jace. She wanted him back like she wanted her next breath.

You have the tools. You have the power.

So what, exactly, was the problem?

Nothing, she thought now, and felt her tears dry up of their own accord. *There is no problem. I want Jace back. I have to have him back. I can't live without him. That's all there is to it. End of story.*

Mind made up, C. K. strode into the kitchen and retrieved the woven basket resting on the counter. She'd thrown this into the dumpster along with the book, just that morning. But now the fact that it had returned was no longer an unwelcome surprise. The basket contained everything C. K. needed to cast the spell that would bring Jace back.

She carried the basket into the living room, then moved through the apartment drawing drapes, snapping off lights. Plunging her rooms into midnight darkness. The drapes behind the coffee table were the only ones she left alone. The light of a nearly full moon filtered in through the window, bathing the leather-bound book in a blue-white glow. The serpent on the cover seemed to writhe in the strange half light, almost as if it were alive.

Carefully now, her movements as controlled and precise as the apartment around her, C. K. knelt on the floor in front of the coffee table and began to remove items from the basket, creating the makeshift altar upon which she would perform her spell.

First to go into position was a medium-size wooden cutting board. Over this, she placed a scarf of indigo-colored silk, embroidered with gold moons and silver stars. Next came a series of votive candles in clear holders. Black. White. Purple. Blue. Orange. C. K. wasn't sure what the different colors signified. She'd only known, standing in front of the display at the magic shop, that these were the ones she was supposed to buy.

Then came objects from the natural world, the world she must conquer, even if only for a moment, in order to successfully complete her spell.

Bright green malachite, to stand for earth. For air, a tail feather shed by a bird in flight. Water from the San Francisco Bay. A cone of sandalwood incense, its recently-lit tip beginning to glow red, its scent filling the room like a ghostly presence, fire. Over them all C. K. scattered the sharp and tangy spears of rosemary, the herb of remembrance. Now, finally, she needed only one thing more.

In the very center of the board she placed a photograph of a young man, her fingers trembling ever so slightly as she set it in position. He was smiling straight at the camera, his face open and warm.

Jace Fraser. The man she loved. Stolen away from her before his time. Before she was ready.

Not after tonight. Not anymore.

At last, C. K. turned her attention to the book, her fingers reaching toward its cover, then jerking back in astonishment. Heart hammering against her ribs, C. K. gave a strangled laugh, relieving her mounting tension.

I suppose I should be used to this sort of thing by now.

The book was already open, as if it had known the spell she wanted all along.

C. K. leaned forward, studying the pages intently. On the left was an illustration of two figures, their faces hidden, their arms wrapped around one another. So closely joined it almost appeared as if two were one. On the right were four lines of text written in an elaborate hand. Above them was an even more elaborately-penned title:

A Spell to Restore a Riven Heart.

C. K. already knew what *riven* meant. Ripped in two. Torn apart.

Just like her heart since Jace's death. Bringing him back was the only thing she could think of that would restore it, make it whole once more. Taking one last look at Jace's picture, C. K. pulled in a deep breath and began to recite the spell.

> *Breath of air, soul of fire*
> *Grant this night my heart's desire*
> *What once was lost, restore to me*
> *Womb of earth, tears of sea*

As she finished speaking, C. K. felt an incredible burst of power surge through her body. *It's working!* she thought. Eagerly, her eyes searched the room, expecting to see Jace's familiar form materialize at any moment.

Nothing.

No! she thought. *This has to work. It has to!*

Again, C. K. recited the spell. And then again, a third, and then a fourth time. Her hair felt so full of electricity she was sure it was standing straight out on end. The air in the apartment felt close and hot, the way it did before a storm. But there was still no sign of Jace.

As she'd been for the past three hundred and sixty five days, C. K. Piers was all alone.

All through the night, C. K. continued to chant the spell, rocking back and forth on her knees, reciting it over and over as the candles guttered, drowning in pools of their own hot wax, and the moon drifted across the sky. Until her voice grew hoarse, and only her lips moved.

And still, there was nothing. Nothing at all.

Just before dawn, she could stand it no longer. She'd broken every rule in her own book. She'd used her power. Performed a spell. And it hadn't worked. Nothing would ever work. She would be alone forever now.

With a howl of anguish, C. K. swept the elements she'd gathered from her makeshift altar, then heaved the coffee table over, sending the book skittering across the floor. Abruptly, the sight of her clean and tidy apartment, symbol of her barren life, her failure, threatened to make her sick.

I've got to get out of here! she thought.

Staggering to the front door, C. K. yanked it open, sending the chair she'd set against it flying. She never heard it crash back down, because by then she was completely out of control. Slamming the door behind her, she ran as fast as her weary legs would carry her into a cold, gray San Francisco dawn.

Inside the apartment, all was still. Though weak morning light was just beginning to spill in through the open curtains, the corners, the nooks and crannies, were still ruled by the shadows, by the dark. Most people assumed that midnight was the most frightening, the most dangerous time. The time when the dark was strongest, because it was most prevalent.

Most people were dead wrong.

It was the dark that lingered the longest that had the most strength. The shadows that could be put to flight only by direct sun. Those were the ones a person had to worry about. And there were plenty of shadows in C. K. Piers's apartment.

There ought to be. She'd summoned them.

The book lay where C. K.'s tantrum had left it. Half underneath the couch, its spine was still open. Someone watching might have noticed the pages suddenly begin to fan, as if a breeze were passing over them. And, as the pages of the book began to move, so did the shadows.

Sliding from every corner of the room, they began to swirl around one another like a child's science experiment: tornado in a bottle. Gathering strength, gathering momentum, they completely destroyed the carefully maintained order of C. K.'s apartment. Silk plants overturned. Books flew from the bookshelves. Even the couch moved, slamming back against the wall, revealing the book hidden beneath.

Now, there was nothing between the book and the shadows.

Instantly, they moved to hover over it, and the tornado shape began to transmogrify, flickering through forms so swiftly it was impossible to identify them all. But finally, someone watching might have observed the shadows take on distinctly human form.

As if this was a signal, the book slammed shut. The shadows retained their human form. Someone watching might have seen it hover in the apartment for a fraction of an instant longer. Then, with a howl of anguish echoing C. K.'s own, it rushed straight through the closed front door.

Someone watching would no doubt have noticed the serpent on the cover of the leather-bound book, its jaws open wide in what could only be considered a smile of triumph.

But there was no one to watch. No one to see.

That is, no one alive.

Two

Excellent, Piper Halliwell thought to herself.

Swiftly and efficiently she moved across the kitchen of Halliwell Manor, carrying a hot cookie sheet she'd just taken out of the oven. On its surface rested round disks of freshly baked bread, their tops adorned with what looked for all the world like fingers. Skeleton fingers. She slid the sheet onto its cooling rack, then stood back examining her handiwork.

Definitely a success, she thought. It was hard to find any task Piper didn't enjoy in the kitchen, with the possible exceptions of scouring the oven or cleaning out the fridge, but trying out new recipes definitely topped her list of likes. In honor of Halloween, she'd decided to try a recipe for *pan de muerto*, literally "bread of the dead." A name that explained the bony digits adorning the tops.

In addition to giving her the chance to try

something new, the sweets would serve as an extra treat for the staff at P3, Piper's nightclub. The club hosted a Halloween bash every year that really kept the staff hopping. When the going at P3 got tough, the boss got busy behind the scenes. The treats Piper frequently brought in to express her ongoing appreciation and to boost morale were one of the perks her staff appreciated most.

Satisfied with the results of her latest experiment, Piper removed the pieces of *pan de muerto* from the cookie sheet, then set the sheet itself aside to cool and checked on the one still in the oven. It still had several minutes yet to go. So Piper settled back in at the kitchen table with her cup of coffee and the morning paper, the *San Francisco Chronicle*. She was reading the front page, focusing on an article about a series of strange incidents that had police baffled.

No wonder, Piper thought. Over the last couple of days, several seemingly unrelated buildings and other landmarks throughout the city had all been vandalized in precisely the same way.

Specifically, they'd been melted.

The investigation was ongoing. A thing which could hardly be considered a surprise.

Piper sipped coffee, her brow furrowed as she stared at a series of black-and-white photographs showing the damaged locations. As always seemed to be the case, the disaster had drawn a crowd. It was hard to see specifics through all the people, but even so . . . Piper hadn't lived her life in San Francisco without being aware of what it took to put a building *up* in earthquake territory. Concrete, support columns of rebar as thick as one of her arms.

According to the paper, part of what was hampering police efforts was their inability to come up with something that could literally melt building materials without leaving a trail of clues a mile long. A problem Piper didn't have. She could think of several possible demon-related things right off. But then, she had to figure she had a working knowledge of some things even the most hardened cops didn't.

Piper Halliwell was a powerful witch. Together with her two younger sisters, she was one of the Charmed Ones.

"I really hope you're not planning on handing those things out to the trick-or-treaters tonight," Piper heard her middle sister Phoebe's voice say, as if she and the ringing oven timer were programmed together. "Whatever they are."

"Pan de muerto," Piper said, as she got up to answer the timer's summons. As Piper slid the cookie sheet from the oven, Phoebe slid into her sister's chair, sneaking a quick sip from Piper's cup of coffee.

"That's not the only cup in the house, you know," Piper observed, dealing with the second batch of pastries as she had the first, then loading up the now-cooled first cookie sheet and popping it back into the oven. "And it's not the only coffee. I made a whole pot."

"I'm not awake yet," Phoebe protested, as she snuck another sip. "This is safer. I might spill a full cup. You wouldn't want that to happen, would you? It'd just be one more thing to clean up."

Good-naturedly, Piper rolled her eyes. Ever since they'd been little, she'd been the early riser, while Phoebe had been the one who'd had to be pried out of bed with a crowbar. Even though her sister's body was up, Piper knew it would still be several minutes before Phoebe's brain well and truly kicked in.

"Try this," she suggested, sliding a freshly baked pastry onto a plate and placing it in front of Phoebe. "It ought to help wake you up."

Phoebe had the roll halfway to her mouth before she spotted the decorations. She gave a strangled shriek, then set it back down onto her plate with a *thump*.

"Please tell me those are *not* fingers."

"I can't exactly do that," Piper answered, trying not to smirk. "But I can promise they're not real ones."

Phoebe shuddered. "It's finally happened, hasn't it?" she asked.

"What?"

"You've lost your mind. Too much domesticity. I always knew it would be your downfall."

"Does that explain why you ate the biggest

piece of lasagna last night?" Piper inquired sweetly. "Even bigger than Leo's or Cole's? Afraid it would be your last?"

"It *was* my last," Phoebe declared. "There are fingers on top of my breakfast pastry. After this, how can I trust what might be in the lasagna?"

Piper laughed as she poured herself a fresh cup of coffee. Then, taking pity on her sister, she topped off Phoebe's cup, put the pot back on the coffeemaker, then sat down beside her. Reaching for the pastry, she took a healthy bite, then set it back down on the plate.

"Ewww," Phoebe remarked.

Piper shook her head, her mouth still full but her eyes dancing. "On the contrary," she said when she could speak. "I'd say they're pretty yummy. You've seen *pan de muerto* before, Phoebes. You can get them at Mexican bakeries all over town this time of year. They're a traditional Day of the Dead thing."

The Mexican festival honoring the dead was actually more than a one day event, beginning before and extending after the American holiday Halloween. Though some north-of-the-border folks found some of the traditions, like candy skulls, bread decorated with fingers, and artwork festooned with skeletons, disconcerting, Piper enjoyed them. In particular, she appreciated the festival's emphasis on celebrating the dead. Honoring them. Making them feel welcome.

You didn't stop loving someone just because

they weren't around anymore, and being dead didn't automatically turn a person into a scary monster. Two things Piper's own experiences had taught her.

"That's hardly the same thing as finding them in my kitchen first thing in the morning," Phoebe muttered darkly. But she reached for the pastry and took a bite. She chewed reflectively for a moment, then took another one. "Okay," she said as she popped the last piece into her mouth. "You've sold me. The gang at P3 is really going to go for these."

Piper gave her sister an approving pat on the head. "There, you see?" she said. "A little caffeine, a few carbohydrates, I knew we'd get that brain going."

Phoebe made a face as she hefted her coffee mug. "I just love it when you treat me like a puppy."

Conversation lagged as Piper responded again to the call of the timer and Phoebe worked her way steadily through her cup of coffee. When Piper had finished her tasks, she returned to the table to find Phoebe staring at the same article that had earlier engrossed Piper herself. She tapped one of the pictures with a forefinger.

"Do you get the feeling we should be saying, 'uh-oh'?"

"You bet I do," Phoebe nodded. "Haven't figured out why yet, though. Other than the incredibly obvious the-melting-of-buildings-is-not-to-be-considered-normal."

Piper regarded Phoebe's fingers, fiddling with the edge of the newspaper. "No . . . you know . . ."

"Premonitions?" Phoebe said, glancing up at her older sister with a rueful smile. "Not so far. Sorry."

Each of the Halliwell sisters had a unique gift, a unique power. One which was enhanced when they used their powers in concert as the Charmed Ones. Piper's gift was the ability to freeze time. She could also blow up demons with a flick of the wrist. Phoebe got premonitions which often gave the sisters vital clues to the challenges they faced while fulfilling their primary purpose as witches: protecting the innocent.

In addition to that, with the aid of her fiancé, Cole Turner, Phoebe'd turned herself into a first class fighter. Cole was a former demon, whose original mission had been to destroy the Charmed Ones. Fortunately for all concerned, he and Phoebe had fallen in love, which had effectively put an end to the destruction scenario.

The youngest Charmed One was Paige Matthews, Piper and Phoebe's half sister. Paige's special gift, the ability to orb herself and others, as well as any object she needed, stemmed from her unique background. She was half Whitelighter. The household was rounded out by Piper's husband Leo Wyatt, who was the Charmed Ones' own Whitelighter.

"Do you think I should go visit one of the sites?" Phoebe inquired now. "I mean, how worried about this do you think we should be?"

"Plenty," said a new voice.

Both Piper and Phoebe jumped.

"Does he *have* to do that?" Phoebe complained.

In spite of the fact that she'd jumped just as far as her sister, Piper grinned. "Actually, yes, he does."

Together, the two sisters turned to face the newcomer, Piper's husband, Leo. The sparkling phenomenon that always accompanied the orbing process was just beginning to fade away. Though Leo could, and generally did, enter and exit rooms the same way everybody else did, when he was officially working, consulting with his bosses, the Council of Elders, he orbed in and out. It was pretty much the only way to get where he needed to go.

Now, one look at her husband's handsome face told Piper there was trouble. Though his smile could light up a room, Leo's natural expression was rather serious. At the moment, he looked particularly troubled.

"You know something we should know?" Piper immediately inquired.

"Something," Leo nodded. "Unfortunately, not enough. We need to talk about these melted buildings. The Elders think—"

"Guys!" a new voice interrupted. A split second later, Paige stuck her head into the kitchen. A black witch's hat sat on top of her hair. As if that weren't enough, she'd blackened a couple of teeth and added a wart to the end of her nose. It was plain she was getting into the Halloween spirit in a big way.

"Go for stereotypes much?" Phoebe inquired.

Paige ignored her. "There's something on the news I think you should see," she said, her tone tense. "There's been another melting."

Three

"Police continue to be baffled by the wave of bizarre vandalism sweeping the city," the reporter for Channel 5 intoned. "The most recent target . . ."

The camera pulled back to reveal a tangle of metal that looked like a cross between a new age sculpture and a slag heap.

"Hey!" Phoebe spoke up suddenly. "I know what that is! I mean, what it was. It's—"

"The statue in front of the downtown branch of First State Bank," the reporter obligingly filled in for her. "The damage is believed to have occurred sometime during the night. Today's discovery brings the total of such incidents to three, one each day since October 28th. While police aren't ruling out the possibility of Halloween-related pranks—"

The camera now began to pan across the shocked faces of bystanders as the reporter continued the voice over. It lingered for a moment on the face of a disheveled young woman, whose eyes were glazed, her mouth open slightly, before moving on to the impeccably dressed businessman beside her.

"—there are growing concerns this morning that the incidents are something else, something more. But as to what that something might be, police still refuse to comment. Meanwhile, residents of San Francisco are eyeing familiar buildings and landmarks nervously, wondering whether something in *their* neighborhood will be melted by the time the sun rises tomorrow morning.

"Reporting from downtown, this is Chen Hao, Channel 5 News."

Swiftly, Paige clicked the remote through the other local channels, all of which provided theme and variation on the same report. When it became clear no other information would be added by the media, she switched off the television. As if they'd all gotten the same hidden signal, all three sisters then turned to look at Leo.

"This is what the Elders wanted to see you about first thing this morning?" Piper asked.

Leo nodded.

"How come?" Paige inquired. "Why are the Elders interested in the destruction of a random bunch of buildings and landmarks?"

"Because they don't think it's random," Leo replied.

"I knew it," Piper jumped in, before Leo could continue. She exchanged a significant glance with Phoebe. "Didn't I tell you? I knew this was going to turn out to be an *uh-oh*."

"You told me," Phoebe agreed. She switched her attention back to her older sister's husband. "So I guess the question of the hour is: How big an *uh-oh* are we talking about?"

Leo's already serious face grew even more grave. "Potentially, about as big as it gets."

Paige plunked down in the nearest chair, the action sending the big brim on her witch's hat flopping up and down.

"Uh-oh."

"What's got the Elders so concerned?" Piper asked.

Leo sat down, too, perching on the edge of the couch and leaning forward to rest his hands on his knees. Piper and Phoebe arranged themselves facing him in nearby chairs. Within moments, Leo was the focus of three sets of worried eyes.

"It's what the damaged buildings—statues, whatever—represent, not what they are themselves," Leo answered Piper's question somberly. "The destruction of the first key *could* have been random. The second, coincidence. But the discovery of the third one this morning . . ."

"Wait a minute, keys to *what*, Leo?" Phoebe interrupted. "You're not making any sense. Go back. Slow down."

"Sorry. I didn't mean to get ahead of myself," Leo said. "It's been kind of a weird morning. I've seen the Elders concerned before, of course. I mean, let's face it—concerned is practically their modus operandi. But usually, they have a pretty good handle on what's going on. This time, though . . ."

His voice trailed off as he frowned.

The sisters exchanged glances.

"The keys, Leo," Phoebe prompted gently, after a moment.

"What?" Leo started. "Oh, yeah, the keys. Where was I? The objects being melted aren't important in and of themselves. They're important because they're the keys to a major set of portals."

"Portal. That's a doorway, right?" Paige spoke up.

"Right," Leo said. "Specifically, these portals lead to the spirit world, the realm of the dead. When everything's working the way it should, the realms of the living and the dead are separated by an energy barrier. The only way through the barrier is through the portals. Their locations are pretty apparent on the dead side of things. The keys mark the spots on the living side.

"What the key actually *is* doesn't make any difference. In fact, it's pretty much whatever happens to exist in the same place as the portal. That's why the damage appears random, when, in fact, it isn't."

"So somebody's attacking the portals between the living and the dead right before Halloween," Piper spelled out.

"That's right," Leo said again.

"There's a fair amount of cross-over between the realms at this time of year anyway, isn't there?" Paige asked. "From the dead to the living side of things, anyway. That's the origin of the ancient festivals, as well as the contemporary ones they've evolved into, like Halloween itself. Could what's happening have anything to do with that?"

"It could," Leo said. "According to tradition, October thirty-first, today, is All Hallows' Eve. Contrary to current popular belief, it's actually fairly spirit-free.

"November first is All Saints' Day, when the souls of dead children return to the realm of the living. The adults return on November second, All Souls' Day."

"And by November third, everybody's back where they belong and things return to as normal as it gets," Phoebe wrapped up. "So why attack the portals when the dead are coming and going anyway?"

"That's the first million dollar question," Leo replied. "If I had to make a guess, I'd say it's the *going* part of the equation that the attacks are hoping to change."

Beneath the brim of her witch's hat, Paige's forehead wrinkled. "And you think that because . . ."

"Because the portals are being attacked from *this* side of the energy barrier," Leo said.

Phoebe sat up a little straighter on the arm of her chair. "This side! But that doesn't make any sense! It's more likely that something on the *other* side wants to get back and—I don't know—slam the door behind it. Probably something like a demon."

"That's what you'd think," Leo agreed. "But that isn't what's happening. That's part of what has the Elders so concerned. The attacks are very definitely being initiated on *this* side of the energy barrier, by something very big and bad that the Elders haven't been able to identify.

"Unfortunately, that leaves the motive for the attacks unclear. We really need to figure out what we're up against."

"Sounds like we need to consult the Book of Shadows," Paige said.

"I agree," Leo said. "I'm hoping you and Phoebe will handle that."

"You got it," Paige nodded. "What else?"

"I'll go visit the damage sites, see if I can learn anything more from being there in person," Leo said. "Phoebe, maybe you could call Cole. See if he can think of a demon who might be responsible for what's happening."

"Will do," Phoebe said.

"What about me?" Piper inquired.

"Actually, I think you should go to P3, as usual," Leo said. "You've got a lot to do, and there's no sense in all of us being disrupted until we know more about what's going on."

"Okay," Piper said, as the group got to its feet. "Though I do sort of feel like a slacker."

Leo gave her shoulders a quick squeeze, though his face was unsmiling. "Somehow, I don't think you'll have to worry about that for very much longer."

"I was kind of afraid you were going to say that," Piper said.

For the first time that morning, Leo's expression lightened. "Are you trying to tell me I'm becoming predictable?"

"What do you think? Old married guy," Piper inquired.

Leo's smile flashed across his face.

"Uh-oh."

She was cold. So very, very cold and tired. How long had it been since she had eaten or slept? She could no longer remember. Not that it mattered, anyhow. Nothing really mattered now. Not since she'd tried to use her power and failed so miserably.

Miserable. Yes. That's what she was.

Come on, C. K. Pull yourself together. Don't give up now. You're not finished yet. There's still more to do.

What? she thought as her feet began to move her weary body along the San Francisco sidewalks. What could she possibly have to do now?

Her feet hurt. At some point she could no longer remember, her sneakers had gotten wet and blisters had formed. Her legs ached, as if she'd been walking for days.

What more was there for her to do? Why couldn't she just go home and rest?

No! the voice inside her head commanded, and C. K. felt a sharp pain twist through her body. *You're not through yet, C. K. We're not through. Not yet. You have to keep on going.*

"I will. I will!" C. K. sobbed aloud, unaware of the way the crowds of pedestrians parted around her. No one wanted to get too close to her, in her disheveled state. "I'll do whatever you say. Just don't hurt me anymore."

Of course not, the voice soothed. *I don't want to hurt you at all, C. K. But you leave me no choice when you defy me. I'll make the pain go away. As long as you go exactly where I say, and do exactly what I tell you.*

"I will," C. K. sobbed again. "I promise." She felt the pain vanish abruptly.

There, that's better, isn't it? the voice inquired. *Just keep on going, C. K. It's not far now.*

"But what am I supposed to do?" C. K. wondered aloud.

Don't worry about that. Leave it all up to me. When you get there, you'll know.

Four

"Well," Piper muttered under her breath. "So much for business as usual at the club."

She'd just arrived at P3 to find the whole area in an uproar. Police barricades at the end of the street had provided the first clue that something was wrong. As soon as she'd seen them, Piper'd gotten a funny feeling in the pit of her stomach. A feeling that had her wishing Leo was around. Sure, a police barricade could mean any number of things. It could be something innocent, like a broken water main.

Today might also be the day that pigs actually got to fly, but, somehow, Piper didn't think so. Based on the throngs of people jamming the barricade, she was pretty sure she knew what had happened.

There'd been another melting. That meant another key, another portal. The only question was, where exactly was it?

Acting quickly, Piper whipped the Halliwell SUV into a parking place, beating out a TV van by seconds. Then, she got out and made her way toward the nearest police uniform. It took several minutes of impassioned conversation before the officer agreed to let her through. Not until she'd produced a photo ID to confirm her name was Piper Halliwell had he agreed.

She had a right to go through and inspect the damage from a safe distance, the officer acknowledged. After all, she was the property owner.

Now Piper stood on the street outside P3, hands on her hips, surveying her club. Or what was left of it. The west wall of P3 looked like it had been on the losing end of an argument with the world's biggest, baddest blow torch. Puddled on the sidewalk was a heap of what had been bricks and mortar. Now it looked like lumpy melted wax. In the wall's place there was now a hole.

A really big one.

Fifteen feet if it's an inch, Piper thought as she stared at it grimly. Through it, she could just make out the employees' changing room and a storage area. The rest of the club seemed untouched, as far as she could tell. One thing was for sure, the Halloween party was most definitely off.

Piper looked around. A dozen uniformed cops and a couple of plainclothes detectives milled about in the area between P3 and the crowd control barriers. Several black-and-white units and a Special Investigations Unit van were parked at the far end of the block.

A team of cops was already examining the wall—or what was left of it—snapping pictures, taking measurements, and putting samples of melted bricks into little plastic bags. One stood slightly apart from the rest, barking orders and reading notes from a pad into his cell phone.

Must be the guy in charge, Piper thought. She didn't envy him the frustration he was no doubt undergoing. Would continue to undergo. No matter what they did, the cops were never going to solve this case, nor any of the others like it.

But Piper and her sisters might. In fact, she pretty much figured it was them or no one.

I need to get inside P3, she thought.

Piper walked up to the detective in charge and tapped him on the arm. "Excuse me—" she began.

Clearly annoyed at being interrupted, the detective flipped his phone closed. "You need to keep back, ma'am. This is police business. In fact, how did you . . ."

"It's also *my* business," Piper informed him as she cut him off. For the second time that morning, she opened her wallet to display her ID. "I'm Piper Halliwell," she continued, pointing to herself. Then she pointing to the melted wall. "That's what's left of the west wall of my club. Any idea how long before I can go inside? I need to see if there's any other damage so I can inform my insurance company."

Not to mention see if the mysterious bad guy left any clues behind, she thought.

The detective's tone and expression softened just a little.

"I'm sorry, but I honestly can't say how long that will be, Ms. Halliwell. Not until late this afternoon, I should think. In addition to collecting evidence, we need to verify that the structure is sound. If you'll leave me your phone number, I can have one of my officers keep you informed."

"Thank you. I'd appreciate that," Piper said. She gave the detective the information he'd requested, then, somewhat at a loss for what else to do, walked slowly toward the car. For one brief moment, Piper's mind toyed with the notion of freezing the whole shebang and making a mad dash for the inside of P3. In the next, she'd dismissed it as unworkable. There were just too many people around.

Besides, she thought. Phoebe and Paige were busy consulting the Book of Shadows. Maybe they'd discovered something by now. If Piper was patient, she might have a better idea of what she was looking for when she *could* go into P3.

Opening the door of the SUV, she saw the box in which she'd transported her morning's baking endeavors resting on the passenger seat.

Piper made a split-second decision. Leaning across the driver's side, she pulled the box toward her.

"Ms. Halliwell, I thought I explained . . ." the detective began, when he saw her walking back toward him with a cardboard box in her arms. He stopped when Piper got close enough for him to see the box wasn't empty.

"These were supposed to be thank you treats for my staff," Piper said, summoning up a smile. "They won't be around to eat them, obviously. So, I thought, maybe your team might . . ."

The expression on the detective's face warred between pleasure and suspicion. "I'm sure they'd appreciate it," he said finally. "But making nice with the cops won't get you inside your club any faster, Ms. Halliwell. I just want us both to be clear about that ahead of time."

"Of all the—" Piper began. Then she cut herself off.

Now that she was really focusing on him, Piper could see how exhausted the detective was. The P3 melting made the fourth incident in as many days and, unless Piper very much missed her guess, no matter how much evidence the police gathered, at the end of this day they'd still be no closer to solving the puzzle than they'd been the day before.

At least she and her sisters stood a chance of sorting things out. As far as Piper could see, the police stood none. But they were the ones who'd be feeling the pressure, both behind the scenes and from the public.

Making an extra effort to keep her voice friendly and calm, Piper said, "My staff won't be able to enjoy them today. I was thinking yours might."

The detective heaved a sigh. "I'm sorry if I sounded rude, Ms. Halliwell. It's just—"

"You don't have to explain, Detective," Piper said simply. She shifted her attention to the crowd pressing against the barricade, to the reporters doing stand-ups practically side by side. "To say you're under an enormous amount of pressure would be an understatement."

The detective gave an unamused bark of laughter. "You got that in one. And, to tell you the truth, I've about reached the point where I'll go for anything that keeps my team's spirits up. Thanks, Ms. Halliwell."

He reached to take the box from Piper, settling it into the crook of one arm. With his free hand, he pulled a card from his shirt pocket.

"You can count on us to be in touch about when you can go inside the club. In fact, I'll telephone you myself. Meanwhile, here's how to reach me if you need to."

He handed Piper his card.

"Thank you, Detective . . . Anderson," she said. "I'll be waiting for your call. She extended one hand. Detective Anderson shook it.

"Thanks again, Ms. Halliwell."

"Don't mention it," Piper said. "And, Detective—good luck."

"Well this round of research is going nowhere in a great big hurry," Phoebe commented. She gazed down at the Book of Shadows, her face puckered in annoyance. Over the last half hour or so, she and Paige had pretty much scoured the Book from cover to cover.

And what had they discovered about their unseen adversary?

Absolutely nothing.

Much as she disliked sympathizing with the Council of Elders, Phoebe had to admit she was starting to understand their concern. How on earth could you discover how to defeat something when you didn't even know what you were fighting?

"Where's a little old-fashioned good luck when you need it?" Paige inquired. At Phoebe's request, she'd dispensed with her witch's hat. As they'd bent over the Book of Shadows together, the brim kept poking Phoebe in the eye.

"Or a little help from our friends," Phoebe muttered, gazing upward hopefully. Sometimes when the going got particularly tough, the ghost of the Halliwell's grandmother, whom the girls called Grams, appeared to help them. Grams had raised Piper, Phoebe, and their older sister Prue after the girls' mother had died. Her help was always useful, but she only intervened when circumstances were pretty dire.

In spite of the fact that she'd all but asked for it, Phoebe was actually of two minds about whether or not she wanted Grams's help now. If she did assist, it would mean the worst fears of Leo and the Council of Elders were justified.

Often, Grams's help came in the form of providing a hint from the Book of Shadows, its pages turning to an entry Grams wanted the girls to be aware of. She didn't always appear herself. But Phoebe's mention of extra help elicited no change in the Book. It stayed open to the page where Phoebe had stopped her search.

Okay, she thought. *Get over your frustration and use your brain, Halliwell.* The fact that Grams hadn't answered her call gave Phoebe information in and of itself. Grams seldom provided assistance if she thought the girls already possessed some portion of the information they needed. It was right in keeping with the way she'd raised them: to be self-reliant. To think for themselves.

"No extra help today, huh?" Paige inquired.

"Nope," Phoebe said. But her tone was re-energized, positive. "Though, actually, I suppose you could say that no help *is* help, if you know what I mean."

"Actually," Paige said. "That would be a great big *no*."

"Grams must think we already know something that can help us," Phoebe explained. "Maybe we've just been going about this search thing wrong. We've been looking for what we *don't* know, right?"

"Right," Paige agreed.

"So, maybe," Phoebe continued, "we should focus instead on what we *do* know."

"Which would be what, exactly?" Paige said. "Other than not a whole heck of a lot?"

Phoebe considered for a moment. "Well," she finally said. "We know that there's melting involved. But somehow that seems more like a means to an end than the key to solving the puzzle."

"Wait a minute! That's it! We know that everything that's been melted so far is a key," Paige cried. "A key to a doorway between the living and the dead. What was it Leo called it?"

"A portal."

"That's right," Paige said. "So . . ." All of a sudden, her voice trailed off. The Book of Shadows had begun to move, its pages flipping quickly all on their own. Now that the girls had figured out the direction in which to search, it seemed that Grams was helping after all.

"I'm thinking this is a good thing and a bad thing," Paige murmured under her breath, as she watched the pages turn.

"And I'm thinking you'd be right," Phoebe replied. As quickly as it had begun, the page-flipping ceased. The Book of Shadows lay still. "Thanks, Grams," Phoebe said. Then she leaned over the open pages. "Okay. Let's see what we've got."

The shadow moved through the streets of San Francisco. Quiet. Stealthy, now. One moment it was thick as soup beneath the boughs of a tree whose leaves had not yet fallen. The next, thin as a trickle of water in the angle where a tall building intersected a midday sidewalk.

Only once did it attract attention, when a toddler, jostled backward, put one foot upon it as it slid along the pavement of a playground. At once, the child burst into tears. It sobbed so wildly, with no end in sight, that the alarmed baby-sitter at once bundled the child up and took it home.

The shadow waited until the crisis had passed, then moved on. Quiet. Stealthy. It searched the streets of San Francisco, seeking the one it had been summoned to find.

Five

"Ms. Halliwell. Ms. Halliwell!" the reporter shouted right in Piper's face, all but shoving a microphone down her throat. "Our sources inform us your property is the site of the most recent incident. Do you have any comment on the damage to your club?"

"Well, I'd say the Halloween party's definitely been canceled," Piper replied.

I suppose I should have expected this, she thought. No sooner had she stepped outside the police barricades to head for the SUV and home, than she'd been surrounded by reporters. The miracle was that she'd been able to get to her car without being stopped the first time around.

"You spent quite a while conferring with Detective Anderson," a second reporter commented now. "Does this mean you have concerns about how well the police are doing their jobs?"

"No," Piper said, as firmly as she could. "It most certainly does not. I'm sure Detective Anderson and his team are doing everything they can in a difficult situation. Now, if you don't mind, I'd like to go home. As I'm sure you can imagine, I have lots of details to attend to."

Without another word, Piper pushed her way aggressively through the sea of reporters, climbed into the Halliwell SUV, and slammed the driver's door. Then she turned the key and gunned the engine, momentarily drowning out the sound of reporters' voices, still calling to her from outside the car. She put the car into reverse and tapped her horn, alerting the reporters that *she* intended to move, whether they moved or not. She was just turning her head to glance back over her shoulder before easing the SUV from its parking spot when a movement at the police barricade caught her eye.

The sound of her horn had apparently startled one of the spectators, a disheveled young woman. She spun toward the sound. For a fraction of a second, she and Piper made eye contact, and Piper felt a sliver of ice slide right down her spine. The young woman's face was haunted and desperate. Not only that, though she couldn't place quite where, Piper was pretty sure she'd seen her before. But before Piper could even begin to put it together, the young woman bolted, pushing away from the barricade and vanishing down a nearby alley.

Her careful movements with the car completely at odds with her racing thoughts, Piper maneuvered the SUV from its parking spot and headed for home. She'd only gone a couple of blocks before a sparkle of lights commenced in the passenger seat beside her. A moment later, Leo orbed into view.

"Anything?" Piper asked.

Leo shook his head. "Nothing. I don't know if it's that there's nothing to find, or that the trail is cold. I got your psychic message, by the way." He reached to squeeze one of Piper's hands where it gripped the steering wheel. "I'm sorry about P3. How soon can we get into the club?"

"Not until late today," Piper informed him.

"Do you want me to try now?" Leo asked.

Piper negotiated a turn before she answered. "No," she finally decided. "I think it's too risky. Too many people around. Let's wait until the police give us the thumbs up. Then, we can all go in together. Meanwhile . . ."

As she maneuvered her way through the San Francisco streets, Piper told Leo about the young woman at the police barricade.

Was Piper's sense of déjà vu about her important, or not?

"A Ward!" Paige exclaimed irritably. "What's that? How come there always seem to be at least six names for the same thing around here? Doesn't anybody in the magic kingdom know that the shortest distance between two points is a straight line?"

Though privately she had to admit she'd often felt the same frustration, particularly in the early days of being a witch, Phoebe patted her younger sister's arm consolingly.

"Down, girl. Remember, the Book of Shadows is on our side. Now take a deep breath, and let's focus on what this page can tell us, all right?"

"All right," Paige huffed. "But I reserve the future right to whine."

"Understood," Phoebe said. She began to read aloud.

"WARD: A grouping of portals or doorways through the energy barrier which maintains the balance between the realms of the living and the dead. While individual portals occur throughout the world, Wards occur only in places of significant psychic activity. For this reason, they are particularly important."

"Sounds pretty much like a fancier way of saying what Leo said this morning," Paige commented. "Except for the part about a Ward being more than one portal. Guess that makes San Francisco a site of significant psychic activity. Why is *that* not a big surprise?"

"Because it isn't," Phoebe answered shortly. "Lighten up, would you please? There's a lot of info here we haven't covered yet. Grams wouldn't have directed us to this page just to tell us what we already know."

"Right," Paige said. "Sorry. Attitude adjustment currently under way."

Phoebe rolled her eyes.

"Though the *function* of portals is universal, to act as doorways, they operate differently in each of the two realms," she read on. "For the dead, the portals are permeable. The dead may pass through them, particularly if invited or summoned. But except for certain times of the year—"

"Like say, for instance, starting tomorrow on All Saints' Day," Paige put in.

"For the living, portals are *not* permeable. They are closed. In this way, the dead are permitted to visit the living when the time is right, but no living person may enter the realm of the dead before their appointed time."

"Man, I've never seen anything in the Book go on this long," Paige said. "Are you making this stuff up?" Phoebe glared at her. "Then again," Paige offered, eager to make amends, "I think I'm starting to get the picture. Read on."

"Portals may be damaged by psychic energy. The type of damage depends on the realm in which the attack occurs," Phoebe continued. "Damage from the realm of the dead will result in a portal being open to anyone, living or dead."

"Don't tell me," Paige put in. "Damage from the living side of things permanently shuts things down."

"That seems to be correct," Phoebe said, her eyes quickly scanning down the page. "Damage a portal in the mortal plane and nobody gets through at all. Any dead who happen to be visiting can't get back home. Uh-oh."

"What now?"

"I think they saved the worst for last," Phoebe said. "Listen to this: Particular concern should be paid to damaged *Ward* portals. If too many portals in a Ward become damaged, the entire Ward may fail. This in turn may cause the permanent disruption of the energy barrier which maintains the living/dead status quo."

"And look, it works the same way individual portal damage does," Paige said, pointing, her attention totally on the Book of Shadows now.

"Destroying Ward portals from the dead side will leave the energy barrier open to the living *and* the dead. Destroying them on the living side will seal the barrier closed. Either way, the result sounds like the end of the world as we currently know it."

Phoebe nodded in agreement. She repeatedly thumped her forehead with the heel of one hand.

"We have more information than we did a few minutes ago, so why don't I feel like I know any more? I just don't get why a demon would want to damage a Ward. Why would it want to seal the energy barrier closed?"

"It wouldn't," said a new voice.

Phoebe and Paige jumped, then spun around to find Cole leaning in the open attic door.

"What is it with the guys in this household?" Phoebe complained. "First Leo, then you. What did you do, take some sort of male bonding sneak-up-on-the-females seminar?"

"Good morning to you, too," Cole said, as he advanced into the room. He dropped a quick kiss on Phoebe's scowling mouth. "Just for the record, I'd say your brain is working fine."

Phoebe's scowl diminished slightly. "Then how come I can't figure this out?"

"Because you're trying to make the facts fit a pre-conceived notion," Cole said.

Phoebe's eyebrows shot up. "Oh, really?" she inquired.

Cole's eyes twinkled briefly, then grew serious once more.

"Think about it for a minute," he advised. "You wanted to know what kind of demon would want to destroy a Ward from the living realm. I can't think of a single one who would, and, frankly, I ought to know. If the Ward that exists here in San Francisco fails, *nothing* is going to get in or out of the living realm. That's hardly in a demon's best interest."

"But that would mean . . ." Phoebe began.

"It would mean that whatever's attacking the portals isn't a demon, but that it is currently present in, though probably not a member of, the realm of the living," Cole finished up.

"I'd say it means something else, too," Paige put in. "It wants to stay here. For a really long time."

Six

I can't *do this. I can't go on.*

Halfway down the alley into which she'd so precipitously fled, C. K.'s energy failed her. It was almost as if she could feel it seeping from her body. Leaching away like water being sucked up by parched ground. In its place came an exhaustion so complete her legs simply folded up beneath her. She sat down, hard, on the cement, too tired to feel its damp and cold.

What am I doing here? Where is here? she thought.

So many things seemed to be gone, missing from her mind.

Her apartment. She thought she remembered being there, running out, though she couldn't remember how long ago that was. She remembered she'd been doing something she knew she shouldn't. Something she'd known was wrong, but that had nevertheless been so very much what she wanted that she'd gone ahead and done it anyhow.

But what had happened after that was one long blur, punctuated by vague memories of walking and walking, and of a pain so great her mind shied away from it, even now.

I'm going crazy, she thought. *It's the only reasonable explanation.*

With a sob, C. K. pressed her hands to her mouth.

I don't want to be crazy, she thought. *But if that's what's happening, why can't I just go all the way and stay there? Why am I remembering all this now? Why couldn't I have just stayed numb?*

It had to have something to do with the woman. The woman in the SUV. The one who'd met her eyes.

In all the days since C. K. had fled from her apartment, no one had done that. It was as if her disordered state, instead of making her more visible, had rendered her invisible. Turned her into someone it was safer not to notice. The glances of passersby had flicked over her, then darted away. Crowds had parted, flowed around her.

Not one person had met her eyes.

But the second the woman in the SUV had done so, C. K.'d felt a jolt shoot through her. For the first time in days, it seemed to her that she came back to herself. That she truly inhabited her own mind and body. The sensation had terrified her. And so she'd done the only thing she could. She'd run, only to collapse moments later halfway down the alley.

She stared down at her filthy hands now. Her usually manicured fingernails were torn and broken. Her clothes looked so disgusting she didn't even want to think about where she'd been. What she'd done.

What have *I done?* she thought. This time, she didn't try to hold back the sobs. What was happening? Had been happening? And what did she have to do to make it stop?

Still sobbing, C. K. began to rock back and forth. More than anything else, she wanted to wake up in her own clean bed, knowing everything was in its proper place. Everything was going to be all right.

Wake up. That's it, she thought. Maybe, if she could only sleep, then she could wake up and the nightmare into which she'd strayed would all be over. The only problem was finding a safe place. She didn't know where she was, but even if she was close by, C. K. didn't think she had the strength to make it back to her apartment.

Without warning, a door slammed open and voices sounded in the alley. Quickly, fear giving her a burst of energy she hadn't known she possessed, C. K. scrambled to get behind a big green metal dumpster. As she scrunched into place, she caught a flash of dark blue. Police uniforms.

"Whaddaya think?" the first voice asked as

two officers stepped out into the alley.

"Well, that outer wall's a pretty big mess," the second voice said. "But the rest of the structure's sound."

"Yeah, but whaddaya *think*?" the first voice queried again.

The second officer laughed, shortly. "What I *think* is that this whole deal is just plain wacko. Like those crop circles in England nobody could figure that turned out to be some great big practical joke. That's what we're going to find out this is. Some weird Halloween thing. I'd hate to be in the perp's shoes when Anderson gets a hold of him."

"Meanwhile, I bet the owner of P3 isn't laughing," the first cop commented.

The second cop snorted his assent. "You got that in one."

"We'd better go give Anderson the all-clear. After that, I could really go for a donut," the first officer went on.

"Hey, I hear the club owner dropped off some kind of pastries or something . . ."

"Maybe she's sweet on Anderson."

"Oh, yeah. That'll be the day."

The voices of the officers faded as they moved off down the alley.

As soon as they were out of sight, obeying some impulse she didn't even try to name, C. K. Piers pulled herself to her feet, and made for the door they'd neglected to lock behind them.

Seven

"So the consensus is what?" Piper asked several hours later as she maneuvered a push broom across the floor of P3. "We're dealing with a seriously disturbed ghost?"

"Well, it would make sense," Phoebe said from the far side of the room where she and Paige were stacking tables and chairs. "Particularly if it's the spirit of someone who died suddenly or by violence. Or both."

"However it got dead," Paige put in, "it's pretty obvious it doesn't want to *be* dead. Trying to destroy the Ward from the realm of the living definitely makes sense if we're dealing with a spirit that's crossed back over to the living side."

"And wants to make sure it stays on a permanent basis," Phoebe wrapped up.

Paige finished hoisting the last chair into place, then wiped her hands on the front of the sweatshirt she'd put on in exchange for her witch's outfit. "Talk about a whole new meaning for the word denial. Just in case anybody's interested, I am now, officially, a mess. Who knew cleaning up a melting was going to be so dusty?"

"The destruction of property is never pretty," Piper intoned. "And that is a direct quote from my insurance agent, just so you know."

"Bet that made you feel a whole lot better," Phoebe remarked.

Piper pushed the broom over to where her sisters were standing. "Actually, it did," she said. "But that was probably because she said it right after she informed me I was covered."

"Your insurance policy covers meltings?" Paige inquired.

"It covers damage due to vandalism," Piper corrected. "That's what the police are calling this, and I'm not about to argue. Especially if it means getting reimbursed for the stuff Cole and Leo are out buying. Speaking of which, shouldn't they be back by now?"

While the sisters checked and cleaned up the inside of P3, Leo and Cole had taken the SUV and headed to the nearest lumber yard for supplies to repair the damaged wall. It wouldn't be a permanent fix, but it would prevent vandalism of the more usual kind.

As if on cue, Piper heard the familiar rev of the SUV's engine, followed a few moments later by a clatter that sounded exactly like boards being unloaded.

"Put this away for me, will you, Phoebes?" she inquired. She thrust the handle of the push broom in Phoebe's direction. "I want to go check on the guys."

"Okay," Phoebe said. Personally, she had to figure Cole and Leo were perfectly capable of unloading the SUV all on their own. One look at Piper's worn-out face and she decided to keep her opinion to herself, though. The club was Piper's baby, never mind that it was also a portal. As far as Phoebe was concerned, Piper was entitled to fuss over P3 all she wanted.

"Remind me where it goes?"

"In the broom closet!" Piper called back over her shoulder.

Paige choked off a laugh. Phoebe stuck her tongue out at her. "*Which* broom closet?" she yelled. She knew for a fact there was more than one.

"The one in the very back," Piper called. "The walk-in one where we keep the cleaning supplies."

"You could always just ride it on back," Paige suggested.

"What is it with you and the witch stereotypes today?" Phoebe asked.

Briskly, she walked to the back of P3, heading for the big storage closet. The push broom had been leaning against the bar when the Halliwells had arrived, most likely placed there by some member of the police team. If left to her own devices, Phoebe probably would have just put it right back where they'd found it. It was likely to be called into service again in the pretty immediate future anyhow.

But she supposed she could understand Piper's desire to have the broom put away. Anything that could be, should be put in order.

The light switch for the storage closet was just outside the door. Nudging the switch into the *on* position with the end of the broom handle, Phoebe reached for the door handle just as the door swung outward toward her, moving with incredible force. Phoebe cried out, releasing her hold on the broom. It clattered to the ground.

"Phoebe—what the?" she thought she heard Paige say. Then she was lost to her surroundings.

Dozens of images rushed through her. The air was filled with the sound of hundreds of eerie voices, crying out in fury and despair. Phoebe caught a glimpse of clipped green grass. Headstones.

Ghosts, she thought. She was hearing the cries of spirits trapped on the wrong side of the energy barrier, unable to return to the realm of the dead where they rightly belonged. In their madness, they began to destroy the world of the living. Trees uprooted and flew through the air. Birds tumbled from the sky.

And then a new set of cries filled the air as the dead began to turn their fury upon the living themselves. Crawling over them like ants over sugar. Biting. Scratching. Clawing. Tearing them apart.

And in the center of it all . . .

As swiftly as it had come on, Phoebe's vision winked out. She was back in P3, hanging onto the storage closet door. For just an instant, a pair of terrified eyes looked straight into hers. Then the girl on the other side of the door gave it a second shove. Phoebe stumbled back.

Behind her, she could hear Paige's startled exclamation. Though her knees were shaking, Phoebe spun around.

"Stop her!" she shouted. "Don't let her get away. She's important!"

"It's all right," she heard Cole's voice come back. "I've got her."

With Paige just ahead of her, Phoebe sprinted for the gap in the wall. The unidentified young woman stood just inside P3, struggling in Cole's arms. He held her tightly, but as gently as he could.

"It's okay. Nobody wants to hurt you," he said. "Just calm down."

"Let me go!" the young woman demanded. "You can't keep me here. I haven't done anything wrong."

"I wouldn't be too sure about that," Phoebe said.

"Phoebe, what in the world?" Piper hurried around the SUV, Leo at her side. At the sight of the young woman still struggling in Cole's arms she stopped short.

"Wait a minute!" she exclaimed. "You were here before. I know you!"

Abruptly, the young woman's demeanor changed. Tears began to stream down her dirt-streaked face. She stopped struggling and stood still in Cole's arms.

Cole shot Phoebe a quick warning look. With a tiny nod of her head, Phoebe acknowledged what Cole was trying to tell her. The change could be a trick, a ruse to catch them all off-guard. Phoebe transferred her weight to the balls of her feet, getting ready in case the young woman decided to try and break free and run. But the young woman's next words had her relaxing again.

"You know me?" she whispered, her enormous, haunted eyes fixed on Piper. "How?"

"You were here before," Piper said again. "I saw you."

"Do you—" The young woman broke off. She ran a tongue over chapped lips, then tried again. "Do you know my name?" she inquired.

Beside her, Phoebe heard Paige make a distressed sound.

"No, I don't," Piper said, her voice steady and kind. "I don't really know you that well."

In the blink of an eye, the young woman's demeanor changed again. Tears still streaming down her cheeks, she began to laugh, wildly.

"Neither do I," she said.

Then her eyes rolled back, and she fainted dead away in Cole's arms.

Eight

"How is she?" Cole asked as Paige came down the stairs of Halliwell Manor.

Though Paige had naturally made the mysterious young woman her first priority, she'd also taken time to change out of her cleaning clothes. Now she was attired in a long black dress with a high neck and lacy long sleeves. She carried her floppy-brimmed witch's hat in one hand. It was apparent she still hadn't given up on the idea of a Halloween costume.

"Sleeping," she answered quietly. "After she finished with her shower, I gave her a clean set of clothes and put her to bed in my room. Leo's with her, working a little Whitelighter mojo. He's hoping a healing sleep will help make her more coherent."

"Good," Phoebe said shortly. "That way maybe she can tell us just what's going on. How long does Leo think she needs to sleep?"

"He didn't actually say," Paige replied, her brow wrinkling ever so slightly at Phoebe's curt tone. "He just said he thought she was completely exhausted and that sleep would be the best thing for her. Though I do think he's hoping his Whitelighter powers can speed the process along. Where's Piper?"

"Laundry room," Phoebe answered, her tone still abrupt. "Personally, I'd have built a bonfire for those clothes."

Paige chuckled and perched on the arm of the couch closest to Cole.

"Let's hope she's one of the good guys," Phoebe said. "That was one ugly premonition I got when I touched the same door she did."

"Well, she hasn't thrown any fireballs, so I'm willing to give her the benefit of the doubt," Paige offered.

"You're right. You're absolutely right," Phoebe agreed. "It's just—" She broke off, her eyes focusing on something Paige and Cole couldn't see. "I know what's going to happen if the Ward is destroyed. I *saw* it. That's what my vision was. The dead are *not* going to be happy campers, and that's putting it mildly.

"That girl upstairs is our only real clue. We've got to find out what she knows."

"Well, at least now *we* know who she is," Piper's voice said as she came into the room.

"We do?" Paige exclaimed. "How?"

Piper extended one arm. The plastic insert

from a wallet dangled from her outstretched fingers.

"Because I found her driver's license in her back pants pocket," she announced. "And according to it, our mystery guest's name is Claire-Kathryn Piers. Apparently, she goes by C. K."

"And you know that because . . . ?" Phoebe inquired.

"Because it's the way she signed her license," Piper said simply.

For the first time since coming home from P3, Phoebe's face relaxed into a smile. "Way to go, Sherlock."

Piper smiled back. "Why, thank you, Watson. Further use of my incredible powers of observation tells me she lives in the Fillmore."

"So she's not a street person," Paige filled in.

"I don't think so," Piper replied. "My guess is that the condition in which we found her has to do with some current crisis in C. K.'s life."

"And her crisis is linked to *our* crisis," Phoebe said. "In fact, it probably caused it."

"Probably," Piper said. "I've also finally figured out why I thought I might know her. Remember that article about all this in the paper this morning?"

Phoebe nodded.

"Check it out." Piper extended the folded up newspaper she'd tucked beneath her other arm.

"It's C. K.," Phoebe said, as she studied the photos.

Piper nodded. "She's definitely in the photographs of the first two damage sites," she said. "And I'm pretty sure I saw her on the TV coverage of the third site this morning. Add to that the fact that she turned up at P3 . . ."

"So she's definitely connected to whatever's going on," Cole put in. "But how?"

There was a moment of silence amid the continuing tension. Phoebe resumed her pacing, in a less agitated way. Piper sat down in one of the living room's overstuffed chairs, her fingers drumming absently along the arm.

Before anyone could speak, the doorbell rang, startling everyone except Paige. She seemed to be expecting it. Setting her witch's hat in position on top of her head, she strode to the front door.

"Trick-or-treat!" The sound of young voices filtered through to the living room as Paige opened the door.

Paige made appropriate exclamations over costumes, dispensed candy, then returned to the living room when her task was done. She had a pleased expression on her face.

"You're really getting into this Halloween thing, aren't you?" Piper observed with a smile.

"Hey," Paige said, as she did a quick twirl around. "You see before you a witch in a witch's costume, modified, admittedly, handing out Halloween candy. What's not to like?"

Even Cole chuckled. "I have to admit, you've got a point."

Paige took a quick bow.

"Much as I hate to rain on the Halloween parade," Phoebe said. "Do you suppose we might get back to the matter at hand?"

"Right," Paige said. "Playtime over, until the next time the doorbell rings, of course. So," she resumed her perch beside Cole. "Where were we?"

"Trying to figure out the link between C. K. and the destruction of the portals," Phoebe reminded her.

"Well, the evidence seems to indicate we're dealing with a ghost, right?" Piper asked. "And *she's* obviously not one."

"No, but somebody important to her sure could be," Paige filled in.

"So the next question is," Phoebe continued, "how on earth do we find that out?"

"I can answer that question," a new voice said.

C. K. Piers stood in the entryway of the living room, Leo at her side.

"Jace Fraser, my fiancé, died almost exactly a year ago," C. K. said in a quiet, strained voice.

Upon her arrival, Cole and Paige had relinquished the couch to C. K. and Leo, who now sat side by side. From across the room, Piper watched the interaction between the two of them with interest. Though C. K. was obviously still under an enormous strain, she no longer seemed exhausted. Not only that, she was coherent. Very definitely a plus.

It was also plain she preferred to stick pretty close to Leo. Not in a clingy, artificial sort of way. More like a plant turning instinctively toward the sun. Leo's Whitelighter mojo, as Paige had called it, seemed to have done the trick, at least partially restoring C. K. to herself.

From across the room, Piper met his eyes, the approval warm in her own. *Well done, sweetie*, she thought. Leo gave her a swift smile. Then he turned his attention back to C. K., his expression sober.

"We're all very sorry for your loss."

"Thank you," C. K. said. She sent a quick, nervous glance around the room, her eyes sliding away when they encountered Cole. He'd put himself as far away from her as possible. Not for his own sake, Piper thought, but for C. K.'s. Now he stood on the far side of the living room, beside the chair that Phoebe had chosen.

"You're all being so nice," C. K. went on. "I don't know if I would have been, under the circumstances. Whatever they are."

"You still don't remember how you came to be at P3?" Piper asked.

C. K. shook her head. "Not clearly, no. I do remember walking—it seemed like forever." Her forehead wrinkled in concentration. "But

I'm not sure I remember exactly why."

"That's okay, C. K.," Leo said. "When you're ready to remember, you will."

C. K. sent him a wan smile.

"I bet the, um, anniversary, was difficult," Paige ventured after a moment. "Of your fiancé's death, I mean."

"Yes," C. K. answered. "Yes, it was. I'd been telling myself I was handling it, doing pretty well. But . . ." She broke off, reaching for the cup of tea that Piper had provided. "The truth is, I was lying to myself. I wasn't handling it. Not at all. I guess that's why . . ."

The peal of the doorbell cut her off.

"That's my cue," Paige said. She scooped up her hat and made for the front door.

"Omigosh. You're a witch!" C. K. interrupted.

Paige stopped short. A charged silence filled the room. "Well, sure, I'm *dressed* like one," Paige said, after a moment. "It's costume, for Halloween."

The bell rang again—insistently. "Keep talking," she instructed as she headed for the door. "I'll be right back."

But C. K. was no longer paying attention. She rocked back and forth on the couch, her arms folded across her chest.

"What is it, C. K.?" Leo asked. "Are you in pain?"

Paige returned quietly so as not to interrupt the moment.

"I remember," she whispered. "I remember now. I remember what I did."

The three sisters made swift eye contact.

"What did you do, C. K.?" Piper asked. In spite of the urgency she felt, she was careful to keep her voice calm.

"I can't," C. K. moaned. "I can't tell you. You'll think I . . ."

Paige moved to kneel at C. K.'s feet. "Of course you can tell us," she said. "We're here to help, not judge."

With trembling fingers, C. K. reached to touch the floppy brim of Paige's witch's hat.

"A spell. I did a spell," she whispered. "I tried to bring Jace back from the dead."

Nine

"A spell!" Phoebe yelped.

She shot to her feet. A startled Paige tumbled over backwards. C. K. shrank back against the couch.

Here it comes, she thought.

This was when the yelling would begin. The accusations that she'd done something wrong. More than wrong, not normal. Unnatural. And then, the punishments would start.

At exactly that moment, the doorbell rang again. Paige pushed herself to her feet and made toward the front door, glaring at Phoebe as she went.

"Let's not overreact."

"What kind of spell? What were the words?" Phoebe asked. She tried to be mindful of C. K.'s delicate mental condition, but the memory of her horrendous vision was making her demeanor a little aggressive than she knew it should be. She took a step forward, toward the couch. From behind her, Cole reached to place his hands on her shoulders, halting her progress.

"Okay," he said quietly. "Just slow down. Being confrontational isn't going to get us anywhere."

C. K. stared across the room in surprise. It was pretty clear Cole and Phoebe were a couple. No matter what happened, C. K. would have expected Cole to take Phoebe's side. But his actions could be interpreted as coming to C. K.'s defense. With the exception of Jace, nobody'd ever done that before.

C. K. sat up a little straighter on the couch. "It was a spell to raise the dead," she answered Phoebe. "I mean, that was the goal. I don't remember the exact words. Lots of things since then are still pretty blurry."

Phoebe opened her mouth. Before she could speak, Piper interrupted.

"That's all right, C. K.," she said. "It's hard to remember things when you're under pressure. We know. But there's another question you might be able to answer."

"Okay," C. K. said. "I mean, I'll try."

"What made you think of a spell in the first place?" Piper asked. "It's kind of an unusual choice."

Oh, no, C. K. thought. *I can't explain. I can't ever explain.*

She let her gaze travel over the rest of the

room's occupants. They'd taken her in, she thought. Though frightened at first, C. K. had quickly realized the group meant her no harm. In fact, they were trying to help. But if she told them the truth . . .

"Did you have a reason to think a spell might work?" Leo prompted, when C. K. didn't answer. "Like, maybe, you'd tried that sort of thing before?"

"Never!" C. K. replied at once, shaking her head vehemently from side to side. "If my grandparents had caught me doing something like that they'd . . ."

Oh, great. Now you've done it.

"You were raised by your grandparents?" Piper inquired.

C. K. nodded.

"That's sort of something we have in common, then," Piper went on, as Paige returned from trick-or-treat duty. "Our grandmother raised us."

Though of course she meant just herself and Phoebe, there wasn't any point in going into complicated Halliwell family dynamics now.

The words were out of C. K.'s mouth before she was even aware she'd thought them. "Did she love you?" she blurted out.

"Of course she did," Piper replied, her tone surprised.

An expectant hush fell over the room. In it, C. K. realized she'd changed her mind. She *wanted* to try to explain to these people. More than that, she wanted their help.

"I *think* my grandparents loved me," she began, stumbling over the words ever so slightly. "I mean—I think they tried. They just never got over my father's death. My dad—he was their son, their only child. He and my mom were killed in a boating accident when I was eight. It had been a clear day, but a storm came up. It swamped the boat and they were drowned."

"And so your father's parents took you in?" Leo asked. C. K. nodded once again. "What about your mother's folks?"

"I don't know anything about them," C. K. said. "I don't think they're still alive."

"My grandparents were pretty strict," C. K. continued. "At first, I thought it was just because they were, you know, old. But then I realized it was because of me. Because of things that I could do."

"What things, C. K.?" Paige asked softly.

Here goes nothing, C. K. thought.

"Strange things," she said. "Accidents. Not to people. I never hurt anyone. But, if I got upset, weird stuff just seemed to happen. Like all the doors suddenly locking, or the burners turning on high when nobody had been anywhere near the stove. Once, when my grandparents wouldn't let me make a card to remember my mother on her birthday, I got

really upset and blew out every single window
in the house. That was the day . . ."

C. K. pulled in a deep breath. "That was the
day my grandmother told me I had . . . powers.
Powers people weren't supposed to have.
Powers that weren't normal. She said I was a
witch, just like my mother. That's why my parents had died, she said. It was all my mother's
fault. Because she was unstable, out of control.
She said . . ." C. K.'s voice dropped to a whisper.

"She said my mother had summoned the
storm."

A silence had settled on the room. C. K. stared
down at her hands, afraid to look up and meet
anyone's eyes.

"I had to learn to control myself, my grandmother said. If I couldn't, then she and Grandpa
wouldn't have a choice. They'd send me away to
a place where I'd be locked up. And she said—
she said—once they locked you up, you never
came back out."

"That's terrible!" Phoebe exclaimed into the
shocked silence that followed C. K.'s words.
"More than that, it's wrong. I'm sorry you were
treated that way, C. K. We all are."

C. K. looked up, her face surprised. The last
person she'd have expected to get outraged on
her behalf was Phoebe. She stole a quick glance
around the room. Nowhere did she see the horror and disgust she'd expect. Instead, the faces
of the others all mirrored Phoebe's words.

Outrage. Concern. Sympathy, but not pity.

"I got used to it," C. K. said simply. "Controlling myself, I mean. It got to be second nature, after a while. It was like I learned to put everything I wasn't supposed to feel into this big room with a big, heavy door. I'd slam the door on my feelings, then lock it behind me. It wasn't until Jace that I . . ."

"Tell us about Jace," Piper prompted. "How did you meet and fall in love?"

"We met at the bank where I work," C. K. explained. "I'm a loan officer. I felt drawn to Jace, right from the start. He was so relaxed, so at ease with himself. And he seemed to understand me in a way no one else ever had. When I knew things were getting serious, I tried to tell him about me. I mean, that there was something wrong. But Jace reacted kind of like you did.

"The only thing wrong, he said, was that I hadn't been loved enough. But he was going to take care of that. He was going to love me for the rest of our lives. And he did, it's just . . ."

"He didn't live very long," Leo filled in quietly.

"It was like a nightmare," C. K. whispered. "When he died. Not just because he was gone, but because I couldn't seem to grieve, no matter how hard I tried. It was like everything I felt for Jace was locked up inside that room I'd created for myself when I was a child.

"All my coworkers at the bank, they thought I

was doing so well. But it wasn't that. It was that I *couldn't* feel, like I was frozen inside. Then, I woke up one morning and realized it was almost a year since Jace's death. That was the day I knew I couldn't stand things the way they were anymore."

"So you decided to try a spell?" Leo prompted.

"I don't know that I decided, really," C. K. said. "It's more like the idea just came into my head, and once it did, I couldn't get it out." She looked across the room at Phoebe. "I genuinely don't remember what the words were, or even where I got them. I'm sorry."

"That's okay," Phoebe said. "Do you remember where you performed the spell?"

"In my apartment," C. K. said. "I remember being there. I remember running out. After that, there are only bits and pieces until I woke up here."

"That's okay," Leo said. "That's good enough."

C. K. looked around the room, taking in the sober faces around her, one by one. A horrible fear was growing in the pit of her stomach.

"I did something, didn't I?" she whispered. "Something bad. Something wrong. My grandparents were right about me. I should have been locked up."

"Of course they weren't right," Phoebe said. "But we won't lie to you, C. K. Some very weird stuff has been going on. Weird supernatural happenings are sort of a special interest of ours. We think there's a very good chance whatever's happening is connected to the spell you performed."

C. K. felt her stomach lurch. "Oh, God," she whispered. "Oh, no."

"There's a way you can help us, C. K.," Leo said. "We need to go back to your apartment to see if we can find the spell. If we can find a way to counteract it, we may be able to stop the bad things that are happening, and find a way to help you mourn Jace at the same time."

To her astonishment, C. K. felt tears prick at the back of her eyes. "You ought to hate me," she said. "But you don't. Instead, you're trying to help me. Why?"

"Because help is always better than hate," Piper said simply.

"And because we're selfish," Phoebe added, with a grim smile. "If we're right, if what's going on *is* connected to the spell you performed, then helping you is the best way to help ourselves."

Something about Phoebe's expression had C. K.'s tears drying up before they could fall. The truth was, she was beginning to appreciate Phoebe's head-on approach. It was so very like the way she'd always wanted to be herself.

She stood up.

"Sounds like the first step is getting to my apartment," she said. "I'm ready whenever you are."

Ten

Piper piloted the SUV, weaving through the misty San Francisco streets, following C. K.'s instructions. C. K. herself sat in the passenger seat beside her. Leo sat on the far side. Paige, Cole, and Phoebe sat in the back. In that order.

Though it had initially stayed clear for the trick-or-treaters, the Halloween night had now turned dank and foggy. Just the sort of weather that helped bring out the fear of the unknown, Piper thought.

"How much further, C. K.?" she asked.

"Not far now," C. K. answered quietly.

Piper had thought C. K. might continue to share confidences on the drive across town. So far, that hadn't happened, though. C. K. slumped in the seat between Piper and Leo. Except when she roused herself to give directions, she seemed completely lost in her own thoughts.

And who could blame her? Piper thought. C. K. certainly had a lot to contemplate, most of it not very nice. The thought of what C. K.'s childhood must have been like truly wrung Piper's heart. It was becoming more and more plain that C. K. did indeed possess some pretty major powers. But instead of getting the guidance and support she'd needed and deserved, she'd gotten ignorance and fear.

No wonder C. K. had been so desperate to bring Jace back. The loss of him must have been completely devastating. With Jace's death, C. K. had lost her only support.

At least when Prue died she still had Phoebe and Leo, Piper thought. And then Paige. None of which had stopped Piper from trying the same thing C. K. had: to bring her lost loved one back to life. She hadn't succeeded any better than C. K. had, but at least she'd had someone around to help her manage her grief and move on with her life. With the exception of the current occupants of the Halliwell SUV, C. K. Piers had no one.

"Turn right at the next corner, Piper," C. K.'s voice intruded into Piper's thoughts. "The apartment building is a converted Victorian, yellow with green trim, about halfway down the block."

"Okay," Piper answered.

A few moments later, Piper was maneuvering the SUV into a parking place in the shabby chic section of San Francisco the local residents simply called the Fillmore. In silence, the SUV's occupants piled out of the car. C. K. took several steps toward the building, then stopped short.

"Omigosh, keys!" she suddenly exclaimed. "I can't believe I . . ."

"All taken care of," Piper said as she fished them out of her purse and handed them over. "I found them in the back pocket of your jeans, along with your driver's license."

"I hope you burned those jeans," C. K. remarked as she took both items and headed for the front door.

"I'm afraid we'll have to walk up," she went on, as she unlocked the door, then held it open for the others. "The elevator almost never works, and I'm on the third floor."

"Lead the way," Leo said. In silence, C. K. led them up the stairwell. A moment later, she used a second key to unlock the door to apartment 309. She swung the door open, her fingers searching for the light switch on the wall by the front door. She snapped it on. Bright light flooded the apartment.

It looked as if it had been hit by a tornado.

Table, couch, and chairs were overturned in the living room. Silk plants were upended. Books had spewed out of their shelves. Every single kitchen cupboard stood wide open. Crockery lay shattered on the floor and counter.

"Oh, no!" C. K. moaned.

At once she began to scurry around the living

room, trying to put everything back in order.

"It shouldn't be like this. I'm not like this," she said, kneeling down to scoop a load of books up into her arms. "Things have a place. I pick up after myself. If my grandmother saw this, she'd . . ."

"It's all right, C. K.," Piper said. Swiftly, she moved to kneel beside the young woman, stilling C. K.'s frantic motions by placing her hands on top of hers. "Your grandmother isn't here. Only we are. We don't care that the apartment is a mess."

"That's right," Leo added. "But we do care *why*. I think this mess is related to the spell, C. K. Can you show us where you tried to cast it?"

"Over here, Leo," said Cole.

While Leo and Piper had been comforting C. K., by silent yet mutual agreement, Cole, Phoebe, and Paige had done a quick walk-through of the rest of the apartment. It hadn't taken Cole long to find what they were looking for.

In the middle of the one uncluttered area of the living room floor sat an oversize leather-bound book. There was a serpent embossed on its cover. A grinning serpent, to be precise.

Cole was staring down at it, his expression grim, when Leo joined him. Together, they regarded the book in silence.

"Are you thinking what I'm thinking?" Leo asked after a moment.

"Definitely," Cole replied.

"And that would be, what, exactly?" Paige asked him.

"Uh-oh."

"Okay, wait. You almost never say things like that," Phoebe protested, as she moved to stand beside him.

"Well, I'm saying it now."

"What is it, Cole?" Piper asked as she and C. K. rose to their feet. "What did you find?"

"That," Cole said, pointing down at the book. He turned toward C. K. "Did the spell you used come from that book, C. K.?"

"I think so," C. K. said, her brow wrinkled, then cleared. She began to speak in a quick, agitated voice.

"Yes, yes I remember now! I went to run some errands in Berkeley. When I was finished, I just kind of wandered around. There was this shop that sold crystals and herbs and stuff. I never go into places like that, for obvious reasons. But the next thing I knew, I was inside the door. It was sort of like I'd been called."

"What happened then?" Piper asked.

"Well," C. K. answered. "I think I bought some things. The shopping basket I always take to the market was filled candles and herbs and stuff when I got back to the car. I don't actually remember buying the book, but . . ." Her voice dropped to a strained whisper. "It was in my shoulder bag when I got home."

"Okay," Paige said. "I'd say the creep-out factor on all of that is fairly high."

C. K. gave a nervous laugh. "That's just the start. I thought about taking the book back, but then I was afraid the store owner wouldn't believe me. I was afraid he'd think that I had stolen it or something. Keeping it around sort of creeped me out, so I took it downstairs and put it in the dumpster."

"It came back, didn't it?" Cole asked.

C. K. looked at him in surprise. "That's right! How did you know?"

"Because that's part of how it operates," Cole said, his voice terse. "Part of what it *is*."

"I think I'm going to be sorry I asked this," Phoebe spoke up. "But I guess we have to know: What is it, Cole?"

"It's a collection of spells called *De Vermis Mysteriis*. Mysteries of the Worm," Cole said. "And it's magic of the seriously evil variety."

Eleven

"There are all sorts of legends about the *De Vermis Mysteriis*," Cole went on some time later. "That make all sort of claims about its power."

The group—minus C. K. who was once more asleep in Paige's room, and Leo, who'd orbed off for a quick consult with the Elders—had reassembled in the living room at Halliwell Manor. Before heading back, they'd helped C. K. restore her apartment to some semblance of order.

While it had seemed odd to be performing such mundane tasks in the midst of a crisis, there was no denying it had improved C. K.'s overall frame of mind. The longer she spent with the extended Halliwell clan, the more C. K. seemed to return to herself. On the drive home, she'd remembered the name of the spell.

Besides, as far as the cleanup went, it wasn't as if there was a whole lot else team Charmed could do at the moment. It was ten o'clock on Halloween night. They wouldn't be able to get to the shop where C. K. had found the book until the following morning. She'd remembered the name of that, too: The Seeking Eye.

"But almost all of the legends agree on one thing," Cole went on. "The *De Vermis Mysteriis* possesses unique powers, almost as if it has a mind of its own. Specifically, a mind that wants to control others, to bend them to its will."

"Great," Paige huffed. "Remind me again why we brought it home?"

"Well, at least we can keep an eye on it," Piper said.

"Right," Phoebe agreed. "Always assuming it doesn't decide to go walk about on its own. Didn't C. K. say something about throwing it in the dumpster, only to have it turn up again in her apartment?"

"She did," Cole agreed. "Though, somehow, I have the feeling we don't have to worry about it vanishing at the moment."

"Why not?" Piper inquired.

"Because, unless I miss my guess, it's already gotten what it wanted. A conduit. In spite of the attributes it possesses on its own, at the end of the day, it's just a book. To accomplish its ends, it needs a human through which to channel its power."

"C. K.," Phoebe said.

Cole nodded.

"And that's why she's been at all the damage sites," Phoebe went on. "Because that thing is sending energy through her to attack the portals."

"Makes sense to me," Cole said.

"But *why*?" Piper inquired. "What's it hoping to gain?"

Cole shrugged. "More power, probably. Chaos, most certainly. I don't know, other than that."

Phoebe snorted. "That's not enough for you?"

The response Cole might have made was interrupted by a sparkling on the far side of the room. Leo orbed into view.

"What did the Elders say?" Piper asked as she crossed to her husband and gave him a hug. "Can they help?"

"To tell you the truth, I don't quite know," Leo said slowly.

"*What?*" Piper exclaimed. She led Leo over to the couch and sat down beside him. Leo ran a hand across his face before he answered, as if trying to clear his mind.

"When I told them we'd found the *De Vermis Mysteriis*, they were obviously . . . disturbed. Then they clammed right up. It was almost as if they were hiding something. About the only information I did get confirms that the *De Vermis* is dangerous. Very dangerous. The Elders claim the book has the power to corrupt anyone it touches."

"Probably why they want to stay as far away from it as possible," Paige muttered.

"Well, that's just great!" Phoebe cried, hands on hips. After all the roadblocks they'd tried to throw in the way of Piper and Leo's happiness, Phoebe was not always a big fan of the Elders.

"What about Cole and C. K.? They've touched it."

Leo's brow wrinkled in concentration. "I don't think that's precisely what the Elders meant," he answered finally. "Not touch as in handle. Touch as in use, perform a spell. In other words, no matter what the initial intent, the book will twist the power of the one who uses it to its own ends. Or at least it will try."

"That fits," Cole put in. "It's said that the *De Vermis* can absorb power. That's one of the reasons it's considered so dangerous—and why it's survived so long."

"So it takes over the power of the person who tries to use it, then uses *them* as a conduit to accomplish its own ends," Piper clarified. "Where does that leave us with C. K.?"

Leo scrubbed his hands across his face once more. "I think we have to assume there may still be a connection," he said. "The portal damage didn't begin to occur until *after* C. K. tried to use the *De Vermis*. And let's not forget, the Ward is still functioning. The energy barrier is still open."

"In other words, the big, bad book isn't finished yet," Cole spoke up, his voice grim. "I think it's time we took a look at that spell."

A brief silence fell across the room. All eyes turned to the *De Vermis Mysteriis*, now sitting on the Halliwell's coffee table rather than the one in C. K.'s apartment.

"Oh, man. I *so* do not want to go there," Paige proclaimed.

"I'll do it," said Cole. "I'm the only one of us who's touched the book so far, right? Let's keep it that way, just to be on the safe side. In particular, I think it would be best if you guys," his glance encompassed Piper, Paige, and Phoebe, "kept your distance. I'll bet this thing would just love to get its paws on the power of the Charmed Ones."

"It's hardly safe for you," Phoebe objected. "Besides, Leo said—"

"I know what Leo said. I still want to do it my way. We know some things about how this thing operates, but that's not the same as knowing everything," Cole countered, his tone making plain that, as far as he was concerned, the discussion was over.

"What did C. K. say the name of the spell was again?" he went on. "Wait a minute. I remember."

Cole moved to the coffee table and bent over the *De Vermis Mysteriis*. Gingerly, he opened the cover. Nothing happened. No flickering lights. No sudden wind storm. But, as he began to leaf through the pages, a strange tension began to fill the room. The hairs on the back of Cole's neck prickled, as if his instincts sensed danger all around him.

They were in the presence of evil. There was no doubt about it.

"Here it is," he said at last. "A Spell to Restore a Riven Heart."

At Cole's gesture, the others crowded around to read the words over his shoulder. None of them were willing to pronounce a spell from *De Vermis Mysteriis* out loud.

> *Breath of air, soul of fire*
> *Grant this night my heart's desire*
> *What once was lost, restore to me*
> *Womb of earth, tears of sea*

"Seems pretty straightforward," Paige said finally. "In fact, it's kind of poetic. I guess I was expecting . . . I don't know . . ."

"Something more overtly evil," Piper suggested.

"But look," Phoebe put in suddenly. She leaned over Cole's shoulder, her finger hovering over the page. "It's also pretty ambiguous. See that language there? Asking to restore what was lost covers an awful lot of territory."

Piper nodded. "I see what you mean. So the book tapped C. K.'s powers, then twisted her spell for its own ends. But what are they?"

"Well, I'd say the restoration of something would be fairly key," Paige put in. "Whoops, no pun intended. About the key thing, I mean."

"Consider yourself forgiven," Cole said,

CHARMED

shutting the book with a snap. "Particularly since I think you're right on the money."

"But the restoration of what?" Piper asked.

"We don't know," Leo answered quietly, and looked heavenward. "And I don't think they know either."

"Or they're just not telling us," Piper said.

"What about being restored to life?" Phoebe suggested, her tone thoughtful. "It is trying to destroy a Ward from the living realm, after all. Who actually created the book—compiled the spells in the first place? Do we know?"

"I don't," Cole said.

"Nor do I," said Leo.

"What about the owner of the store in Berkeley?" Paige suggested. "What was its name? The Seeking Eye. He had the book. Maybe he knows its origins."

"Good suggestion," Leo said.

"Particularly since the Elders aren't helping any," Phoebe muttered. "So—we hit the Seeking Eye first thing in the morning. Meanwhile, we'll keep watch over C. K. The worm book isn't finished yet, and All Souls' Day is day after tomorrow. That's when the largest numbers of the dead will cross over to the living realm. We've got to make certain they'll be able to get back. Otherwise . . ."

"I hate to state the obvious," Paige spoke into the brief silence that had followed Phoebe's words. "But shouldn't we be doing more than just figuring out what the book wants? Shouldn't we also be figuring out the way to stop it?"

"Absolutely right," Piper said strongly. She eyed the *De Vermis Mysteriis* darkly. "I don't suppose it could be as simple as destroying it, could it?"

"I don't think you can," Cole answered. "Although I doubt it's ever faced a power as strong as the Power of Three, so it may be worth a shot. But that's all you'll get—one shot. And if it doesn't work, the consequences could be—"

"Don't say it," Phoebe cringed as she cut him off. "Let's think positively. Maybe finding out more about who created it will give us a clue as to how to destroy it."

"Right," Piper nodded. "Positive thoughts only from now on. I don't know about the rest of you, but I'm starting to feel a little punchy. I say we all go to bed and get a good night's sleep. We're definitely going to need to be sharp in the morning."

"No way am I sleeping in the same room as that thing," Paige announced, pointing to the *De Vermis Mysteriis*.

"I'll take it out to the car," Cole promised.

"Meanwhile, I'll go grab some jammies and check in on C. K.," Paige said. "I hope at least *she's* having sweet dreams."

"No kidding," Phoebe muttered, as she trailed Cole out to the car. "At least that would make one of us."

Twelve

THOSE WHO WOULD DISCOVER
WHAT LIES WITHOUT
MUST FIRST UNCOVER WHAT LIES WITHIN
YOUR JOURNEY OF DISCOVERY BEGINS HERE
WELCOME TO THE SEEKING EYE

HOURS, M-F 9A.M.-7P.M. SAT 9A.M.-6P.M.

SUN 12P.M.-5P.M.

"Well, this definitely seems to be the place," Phoebe remarked as she eyed the occult shop's front door.

It was painted bright purple, the lettering done in shimmering gold. In almost any other retail neighborhood, the combination would have stuck out like a sore thumb. Not on a street near the UC Berkeley campus, though. Here, the décor of the Seeking Eye seemed right at home. The neighborhood was colorful, to say the least. Though it was early in the day, craft booths already dotted the sidewalks, most selling wares the colorfully-dressed vendors had made themselves.

"I really hope that's not the owner," Piper remarked as she eyed the suit of armor standing beside the door. Its gauntlet-clad hands held up a sign which proclaimed, COME IN! WE'RE OPEN! It seemed a pretty safe bet to assume the other side said SORRY, WE'RE CLOSED. Someone had perched a propeller-topped beanie on the knight's visor. Strangely enough, it looked right at home.

"Hey, check this out," Paige spoke up. She pointed to a poster in the shop's front window. "'Moona Lovecraft will predict the future by reading your toenail clippings.' I wonder if it makes a difference if they're painted or not."

"Oh, no, I'm sure they have to be natural," C. K. said, her expression serious. "All those chemicals in nail polish interfere with the toenails' natural aura."

Phoebe swung around. These were practically the first words C. K. had spoken all morning. Though C. K. had admitted it made good sense, she'd also been obviously reluctant to return to the Seeking Eye. She'd agreed to come along only when it had been made absolutely plain that staying behind was not an option.

"I seriously hope you're joking," Phoebe said.

C. K.'s eyes twinkled, and her face relaxed into a smile.

She's pretty when she does that, Phoebe realized

suddenly. And she remembered all the reasons
C. K. hadn't done it more. It made Phoebe feel
even more thankful for her own family. And
even more determined to make certain they all
got out of this all right.

Phoebe turned back around and seized the
door handle. "Okay," she said. "Let's go see
what Mr. Wizard here has to tell us."

Paige linked arms with C. K. as they crossed
the threshold. "I think you really had her for a
moment there," she whispered. "Way to go."

The Seeking Eye was small but neat, every avail-
able surface and shelf packed with supplies.
Books about a variety of metaphysical subjects
lined one wall. The opposite one contained
shelves filled with neatly-labeled jars of herbs
and bowls of polished stones.

A long table filled the center area. Altar
cloths, colored candles and incense, and books
of the coffee table variety were displayed on it.
Dozens of sets of wind chimes hung from the
ceiling overhead, tinkling softly as the breeze
blew in from the front door. An indoor fountain
gurgled softly to itself in one corner. The air was
filled with a pleasant, slightly earthy smell.

Not too bad, Phoebe thought. You never knew
quite what to expect when entering an occult
supply store. Some were pretty out there, more
about playing dress-up than serious magic.
Others, like this one, seemed to take themselves

seriously, and their customers as well.

"Good morning, gentle folk. May I be of some assistance?" a voice asked. Phoebe swung around.

Well, so much for the serious part, she thought.

The Seeking Eye's proprietor was one of the roundest men Phoebe had ever seen. A brown homespun robe spanned his ample girth. It was tied around the waist with a rope belt that ended in two Celtic knots. On his feet were a pair of dark brown leather boots. Around his neck hung a heavy chain ending in a symbol Phoebe couldn't identify. In one hand, he carried a staff right out of every illustration of a wizard she'd ever seen.

Phoebe might think he looked like Friar Tuck, but she was willing to bet money the guy himself was aiming more along the lines of Gandalf.

"Are you the owner?" Phoebe asked.

The round man nodded. "Samuel Gibson, Mage of the Ancient Mysteries, Seer of Past and Future, and Wise Wizard of the Greenwood, at your service Madam. Or perhaps I should say, ladies," he corrected, acknowledging Paige, Piper, and C. K. with as much of a bow as his form allowed.

"You were here the other day, weren't you?" he asked, his eyes lingering on C. K. "I hope you were satisfied with your purchases."

"Actually," Piper said. "That's sort of what we're here to talk about."

"Items may be returned for in-store credit or exchange only," the Mage of Ancient Mysteries said promptly.

"We don't want to return anything," Phoebe reassured him. "As a matter of fact, we want to know where *you* got something."

Abruptly, the Wise Wizard of the Greenwood's shoulders sagged.

"You're here because of the *De Vermis Mysteriis*, aren't you?" he said. Without waiting for a reply, he strode to the front door, opened it, and flipped over the sign in the knight's hand. The Seeking Eye was now officially closed.

"I think you'd better come with me," Samuel Gibson said.

"I've been waiting for someone to show up ever since I noticed the book was missing," Gibson explained several moments later.

After locking the front door, he'd ushered his morning visitors into a back office. It was surprisingly comfortable, sort of like an absent-minded professor's study. Currently, they were seated on a variety of overstuffed chairs.

Like the Seeking Eye itself, the walls of Gibson's inner sanctum were lined with bookshelves. But one could tell at a glance that the books stored here were different than the ones out front. Many were bound in leather and appeared to be quite old. This no doubt represented Gibson's personal library.

"Could you tell us how you came by the *De Vermis Mysteriis*, Mr. Gibson?" Phoebe inquired. By unspoken consent, she had taken the lead in the discussion. She was the one who'd had the vision of what the future might hold.

"I would if I could," Gibson replied.

"Don't tell me, it followed you home, right?" Paige put in.

Gibson nodded. "That's about the size of it. I'd heard of the *De Vermis* before, of course. Any serious student of occult manuscripts has. But I certainly never expected to ever encounter it myself."

"And where was that?" Piper asked.

"At the home of Professor Anthony Lawson—perhaps you've heard of him?"

Phoebe shook her head. "Sorry."

Gibson waved a pudgy hand. "That's all right. It's not really important. Until recently, Lawson was a mythology professor at the College."

The College, Phoebe knew, meant UC Berkeley. "Okay," she said. "Please, go on."

"Several weeks ago," Gibson continued. "Lawson surprised pretty much everyone by giving up his position, selling off his library, and moving out of town. Naturally, I went to the sale. Not that I expected to be able to acquire anything. I'm just a small-time collector, really. The prices Lawson was asking were too rich for my blood."

"But the *De Vermis Mysteriis* had other ideas," Paige said.

This time, it was Gibson who nodded. "I bid on it, of course," he said. "But I dropped out of the running pretty early on. I assumed the book was in the possession of the highest bidder, until I got back to the shop. That's when I discovered it was actually in *my* possession."

"What happened then?" Piper asked.

"Well, naturally, I attempted to contact Lawson, to explain the situation," Gibson replied. "The *De Vermis* is reputed to possess several highly unusual qualities. If nothing else, I thought he might be interested to learn that at least one of them was true. He refused to take my calls.

"This went on for several days. To tell you the truth, I was just about at my wit's end, until the day that young lady with you came into the shop. It was at the end of that day that I realized the book had, well, moved on. I assume she's the one who . . ." Gibson's voice trailed off.

"You assume correctly," Phoebe said. She glanced around the room, just realizing C. K. was missing. "Where is she, by the way?"

"I think she's out in the shop," Paige said. "She was kind of . . . you know . . ." She cut her eyes at Gibson.

"She's concerned you might think she took the book deliberately, Mr. Gibson," Piper filled in helpfully.

Gibson snorted. "After what I've been through myself? Not likely. You didn't bring it back did you?" he asked suddenly, as if the possibility had just occurred to him. He sat up straight in alarm.

"No," Phoebe said.

Gibson relaxed once more.

"Do you know anything about the book's origins, Mr. Gibson?" Phoebe asked. "About who created it and why?"

"Yes, as a matter of fact, I do," Gibson answered. He rose and moved to a nearby bookcase, the only one in the room fronted by glass doors that closed and locked. "The history of magic is my main interest, really," he went on, as he removed a spray of dried flowers from a small pitcher resting on top of the bookcase. He upended the pitcher. One dead spider, three dead flies, and one small gold key tumbled out into the palm of his hand.

"I'm not particularly interested in casting spells, myself. But getting a glimpse into the minds of those who do—well, that's another matter."

Gibson set the pitcher back on the bookcase, replaced the dried bouquet, then put the key down beside the pitcher and dusted off his palms. Then, finally, he retrieved the key and inserted it into the lock on the bookcase door. He turned. The lock moved back with a brisk *click*. Gibson opened the door and reached inside.

Somewhat to everyone's surprise, he extracted the smallest book in the case. It was bound in leather. At first, the cover appeared to be unadorned. But, as Gibson moved across the room, the sun glanced off the cover, illuminating more than the leather as the girls got a good look at it.

The book had a serpent embossed on its cover, just like the *De Vermis Mysteriis*.

Not one serpent, but two. Twined around each other until they were face to face.

Gibson resumed his seat just opposite Phoebe, then opened the cover of the book. As he did so, the serpents began to writhe. As the Charmed Ones watched in astonishment, the head of the serpent on the left seemed to strike out in a blur of motion, its jaws completely devouring the head of the serpent on the right.

"Um, Mr. Gibson . . ." she began.

"Yes, my dear," Mr. Gibson said. "You saw right. And it's more than just a macabre decoration or trick of the eye. In fact, you could say it's the history of the creation of the *De Vermis Mysteriis* in a nutshell."

Making concerned eye contact with her sisters, Phoebe pulled in a breath.

"Okay, Mr. Gibson," she said. "Please, tell us what you know."

Thirteen

"The book was created by two brothers," Samuel Gibson said. "Twins, in fact. Identical twins—an aspect of their relationship which is actually quite important and may explain much about the *De Vermis Mysteriis* itself."

"In what way?" Phoebe inquired.

Gibson leafed through several pages, then turned the book he'd taken from his case to face her. Both Piper and Paige moved to gaze over Phoebe's shoulder. In front of them was an image, the bold black and white of its lines suggesting a woodblock. In it were four figures. Or rather, the same set of figures twice.

In one pairing they stood side by side, arms linked together. In the other they faced one another. In both they seemed absolutely alike.

"Who were they?" Piper asked. "Do you know their names?"

"Mileager and Malvolio De Vermis," Samuel Gibson answered.

"De Vermis?" Piper wondered.

"Just so," Gibson acknowledged. "The serpent, or the worm, was their family crest."

"So the Mysteries of the Worm could refer to them, as well as to the book of spells," Piper concluded.

"Exactly," Samuel Gibson said, nodding. "Mileager was the elder." He tapped the figure on the right in both pictures. "By all of about a minute and a half. Sometimes that's all it takes, though."

"Sibling rivalry," Paige spoke up suddenly.

"That's right," Gibson said.

"Not that I—we'd know anything about that," Paige rushed on, then blushed.

Phoebe patted her hand.

"Family dynamics can be complicated, particularly where magic is involved," Gibson said blandly.

Piper chuckled. "You can say that again."

"And the family dynamic between the brothers was what, exactly?" Phoebe asked. "Good twin, bad twin?"

"Right again," Samuel Gibson said. "Though, in all fairness, it didn't start out like that. The brothers were close for many years, until Mileager began to develop an interest in magic. This is his diary, his journal. In it, he records many things, including changes in his relationship with his brother. Becoming adept in the ways of magic made Mileager De Vermis a very powerful man."

"But he was already powerful," Piper said thoughtfully. "He was the eldest."

"Apparently, that's what Malvolio thought," Gibson nodded. "And that's when all the trouble began. The *De Vermis Mysteriis* didn't start out as a work of evil. In fact, it was originally conceived as a work which would have the power to do great good. Mileager De Vermis set out to create a collection of the world's most powerful spells, particularly spells to heal, to restore balance.

"The De Vermis brothers lived in highly uncertain times. The *De Vermis Mysteriis* was going to be Mileager's antidote to chaos."

"A Spell to Restore a Riven Heart," Phoebe murmured.

"Is that from the De Vermis?" Gibson inquired.

Phoebe nodded. "Even if it didn't start out evil, it sure ended up that way," she said. "How?"

"Malvolio De Vermis's jealousy, essentially," Samuel Gibson replied. "The more spells his brother collected, the more Malvolio longed to control them."

"But you don't really control white magic," Piper objected. "Not in the sense of bending it to your will. It's a thing that works through you."

"Well said," Gibson commented. "Unfortunately for his brother, and the rest of the world, Malvolio De Vermis never grasped that point.

He saw magic as a means to an end, and that end was unlimited personal power. Because that's all he saw, he assumed it was all that Mileager saw too. And as far as Malvolio was concerned, his brother already had more than enough personal power.

"So Malvolio De Vermis turned to the only thing he could think of that could counter the spells his brother was collecting and recording. The power of evil. The power of darkness."

"One serpent devouring the other," Phoebe said.

"That's right," Samuel Gibson nodded. "The brothers were almost evenly matched, but, in the end, Malvolio's willingness to do whatever it took to win allowed him to overcome Mileager."

"What happened to him?" Paige inquired. "Mileager, I mean."

"That's part of the mystery," Gibson answered. "Nobody really knows. What is known is that, even in the midst of what was in all likelihood his final demise, Mileager De Vermis managed to spike his brother's guns. Malvolio wanted the power of the book, so Mileager gave it to him."

Swiftly now, Gibson turned to the end of the book, to another illustration. This one showed one of the two identical figures literally being pulled into the pages of an open book. Fury and despair radiated from every line of his face. It was entirely plain that this was not the ending the figure had in mind.

"He imprisoned him inside it," Phoebe whispered.

"Specifically, until the end of the world," Gibson added solemnly. "Mileager himself vanished at almost exactly the same moment. What happened to him isn't known, as he wasn't exactly around to record it."

"That's it!" Phoebe cried, leaping up abruptly. Startled, Gibson jerked back. Only the fact that he was already sitting down kept him from toppling over.

"That's what?" Paige asked. "Geez, Phoebes. Give us all heart attacks, why don't you?"

"That's why the De Vermis is destroying the portals, trying to destroy the Ward," Phoebe went on. "Destroy the Ward . . ."

"And you destroy the world," Piper said softly, her eyes on the final illustration Samuel Gibson had showed them. "Malvolio De Vermis is trying to get out of the book."

A chill wind seemed to slip into the room, almost as if Piper's words had summoned it. From the outer shop, there came the faint sound of wind chimes.

"That's odd," Samuel Gibson said.

"I'd say it's more than that," Phoebe snorted.

"No, I mean the wind chimes." Gibson got to his feet. "I closed the shop."

The same thought seemed to occur to all three sisters at the same moment.

"C. K.," Piper said as she, too, leaped to her

feet. But it was Paige, closest to the door, who was the first to confirm the fear that had suddenly clutched at all their hearts. Reaching the door to Gibson's office in two quick strides, she threw it open.

The door to the Seeking Eye stood open as well. The wind chimes dangling down from the ceiling continued to make their gentle music. They were the only thing moving in the entire store.

Paige turned back to her sisters, her dark eyes wide with concern and alarm.

"She's gone."

Fourteen

C. K. Piers raced down the sidewalk, her body moving as if it had a will of its own. She'd tried to stop, tried not to give in to the demand that she leave in the first place, but every time she tried to resist, a pain as searing as a red-hot poker seemed to bore straight through her skull.

Its aftermath left her weak, disoriented, with only one goal: to do whatever it took to make the pain stop. That meant doing whatever the voice inside her head told her to do.

And what it had told her was that she had to leave the Seeking Eye. There was somewhere else she had to be. Somewhere important. She would be punished if she didn't get there in time.

Faster, C. K. Faster.

"I'm going as fast as I can!" C. K. sobbed. But even as she made the claim, her feet stumbled over a curb.

You think so? the voice inquired.

C. K. could feel the menace in it, soft as velvet, cool and slick as silk, slide right down her spine.

Let's just test that little theory, shall we? the voice suggested.

Desperate to avoid the pain, C. K. somehow forced her exhausted legs to go faster.

That's the spirit, C. K., the voice purred even as C. K. herself, sobbed in terror. *Now, run. Run.* Run!

"We've got to find her," Phoebe snapped. "Now. As soon as possible. Actually, sooner than that, but I'll take whatever I can get."

"I'm thinking scrying spell," Paige said.

"Me, too," Phoebe nodded. "But we need something that belongs to her, something that bears her imprint and can help lead us to her. I don't suppose you still have her driver's license or anything, do you?" she asked Piper.

Piper shook her head. "I gave it all back to her, and her clothes are in the laundry room at the Manor."

"We could orb to her apartment," Paige suggested.

"I hate to interrupt," said a fourth voice.

All three sisters jumped. In their distress over C. K.'s sudden disappearance, they'd forgotten all about Gibson, the Seeking Eye's owner. Now, it was plain he'd overheard every single word they'd said.

"Um, Mr. Gibson, maybe we'd better explain," Phoebe began.

"Oh, there's no need to do that, my dear," Samuel Gibson said. "Particularly as you and your sisters . . . you are sisters, aren't you? I mean, all that talk about sibling rivalry . . ."

Phoebe nodded.

"You and your sisters are obviously in a hurry," Gibson went on. "I wouldn't want to interfere. The situation does seem rather dire. But I wonder if you'd answer just one small question before you go. Am I, by any chance, in the presence of the Charmed Ones?"

Phoebe felt her mouth drop open. Beside her, she heard Piper make an odd, strangled sound. Paige choked back a startled laugh. Phoebe made a split second decision—exactly the type she usually avoided, but the situation seemed to call for it.

"You sly old fox, Mr. Gibson." She winked. "How did you know?"

Gibson's round face glowed with pleasure. "I think I may have mentioned that it's the *history* of magic that's my true interest," he said simply. "And it's filled with mention of the Charmed Ones. I'd even heard rumors that you were alive and well and living in the Bay Area. It's been my secret dream that someday one of you would come into my shop. But to actually have all three . . ." His voice trailed off.

"You *do* understand it's important no one

knows who we are, don't you, Mr. Gibson?" Phoebe asked. "Most people don't have the perspective on magic that you do."

"I understand perfectly," Gibson said at once. "Though, if I might point out—I don't, in fact, know *who* you are. I only know *what*. I don't believe you ever gave me your names, did you? Perhaps we ought to leave things just as they are. Though, naturally, I hope that if you ever need any supplies . . ."

"You'll be our first stop from now on, Mr. Gibson," Piper promised.

"Well, now," Gibson said, his face turning pink. "That is nice. Don't let me keep you any longer. I hope I've been of some help."

"Enormous help," Phoebe said. "Thank you, Mr. Gibson."

Together Phoebe, Paige, and Piper left the Seeking Eye. Leo was leaning against the wall beside the knight.

"Am I ever glad to see you," Phoebe said.

"Hey," Piper protested. "That's my line."

"Mine, too, in this case," Paige put in.

Leo's eyes twinkled briefly in his serious face. "Must be why I got the cosmic vibe. What's up?"

"C. K.'s disappeared," Phoebe said without preamble. "To find her, we're thinking scrying spell. That means we need to get to her apartment and we need to do it now. You take Paige and Piper. I'll raise Cole on the cell and have him meet you there."

"Why don't we all just go with Leo?" Paige asked.

Phoebe shook her head. "Once we locate C. K., we're going to need regular, everyday transport. I'm thinking I might drive around in this neighborhood, while you guys do your thing. She's on foot. She may not have gotten far."

"Be careful," Leo warned.

"I will," Phoebe promised. "Find her, you guys. Come midnight tonight, All Souls' Day begins. There are going to be an awful lot of dead people wandering around. Unhappy ones, if Malvolio De Vermis gets his way. The clock is very definitely ticking and time is not exactly on our side."

"Don't worry, we'll find her," Piper said.

The question was, would it be in time?

High over the city, the shadow writhed, stretching out across the hazy sun like a wisp of tormented cloud. It drifted on the wind, letting the air carry it out across the water.

Searching, always searching. Never doubting it would find the one for whom it searched.

Soon, very soon now.

Fifteen

"Okay," Paige said. "What exactly are we looking for?"

"Something personal," Piper answered. "Whatever we think will give us the strongest connection with C. K." She glanced around the living room of C. K.'s immaculate apartment. "Somehow, I don't think it's in here."

"Bedroom or bathroom," Paige suggested promptly.

"Let's try the bedroom first," Piper said.

Paige nodded. "Gotcha."

"You know, I actually think I could really get to like C. K., aside from the whole controlled-by-evil-powers-trying-to-destroy-the-world thing," Paige said as the sisters entered C. K.'s bedroom. She put her hands on her hips and looked around. "But I have to say, that girl does have some serious issues concerning tidiness."

Like the living room, the bedroom was well

organized and spotless. It hadn't taken long to restore it to its current state, even after the spell that C. K. had performed had released powers that messed up her apartment.

"I don't see a problem," Piper answered. She was something of a neat freak herself and appreciated the tranquility that order brought to life. Not that much remained orderly at Halliwell Manor with demons showing up every day. The one thing that Piper did notice here, though, was the lack of personal mementos. C. K. seemed to possess none, which made the neatness just seem sterile. And made their current task almost impossible.

Then Piper found the one thing that made C. K.'s house a home. An ancient stuffed teddy bear propped in between the pillows on the bed. Though its position was as precise as everything else in the room, the bear itself was not. One ear drooped. Clumsy black stitches had mended one raised paw. The fur on its body was threadbare in patches. In short, it looked old and well loved.

"Teddy bear," she said, just as Paige surged toward it of her own accord. She scooped it up, then carried it to Piper.

"What else?" she inquired.

"Nothing. We orb back to the Manor for a map," Piper said.

Moments later the orb sparkles cleared, and Piper and Paige were in the attic of the Manor.

Piper opened their map of the city. "Let's hope we can find her. I hate to say it, but I'm afraid we're running out of time."

Phoebe piloted the Halliwell SUV through the streets of Berkeley, one eye on the road, the other on the crowded sidewalks. Usually she enjoyed watching the eclectic makeup of the famous college town's citizens go about their various tasks. There were far too many of them to suit her today, though. Phoebe'd tried to be organized about her search, moving out from the Seeking Eye in ever-widening circles.

So far, her search had added up to the shape she was making: a big fat zero.

About the only good news was that she'd been able to get in touch with Cole on his cell. She'd filled him in on what they'd learned from Samuel Gibson, then informed him of C. K.'s disappearance. He was standing by, awaiting further instructions.

Phoebe turned a corner and began another circle. Tension crawled like pinching fingers up the back of her neck.

"Okay," Piper said. "Here goes."

Piper rested on her knees, holding the teddy bear gently yet firmly in her lap. In the hand not grasping the teddy bear, she held a locket on a thin, gold chain. Paige had discovered it on C. K.'s dresser. Piper pulled in a breath, expelled it slowly, then let the locket slip through her fingers until the chain was stretched to its full length and the locket hovered just above the map. Then, closing her eyes and emptying her mind of everything except the task at hand, she began the words of the scrying spell.

> *Beings who see, beings who say*
> *Aid me in this task, I pray*
> *Where C. K. wanders, let me see*
> *As I will, so mote it be*

Almost as soon as Piper finished speaking, the locket began to move, swinging wildly. She opened her eyes. She could feel the chain growing warm within her fingers' grasp. Piper jerked the locket higher.

Then suddenly the chain of the locket snapped taut. The golden heart dangled down. *One, two, three,* Piper silently counted. The chain and locket remained motionless.

Piper and Paige noted the location. They called for Leo.

"I'm calling Phoebe's cell phone," Paige said.

Without warning, the chain in Piper's fingers grew so warm she could barely hold it. Some sort of big-time energy was near the location the scrying spell had revealed.

"Tell her to be careful," she warned.

"She's on the Berkeley waterfront," Phoebe heard Paige's agitated voice sing across the phone. "Piper says—what?"

Paige broke off and Phoebe used the moment to carefully negotiate an intersection. "Piper says remember that funky restaurant Grams would take you guys to sometimes?"

"That seafood place? The one with the best sourdough bread in the whole Bay Area?" Phoebe spoke into her mouthpiece.

"Yeah, that's it," Paige confirmed after a quick Piper consult. "C. K.'s somewhere near there."

"Okay," Phoebe said. "I'm calling Cole. Do you want him to pick you up, or do you want to orb?"

"We're going to orb," Paige said, after a brief pause. "Piper thinks she remembers an alley where we won't be noticed."

"Okay," Phoebe said. "See you there."

She punched OFF, then hit the speed dial for Cole. She relayed directions, her eyes focused on the traffic, her mind trying to calculate what might lie ahead. She took a corner, tires squealing.

The first of the sirens began to wail as Phoebe switched off the phone.

Sixteen

The blast of hot air almost knocked Paige off her feet.

"Piper, for crying out loud!" she yelled.

"Give me a break," Piper protested, lifting an arm to shield her face. She, Leo, and Paige were standing in the mouth of an alley between two warehouses. Directly across from where they stood, another warehouse was burning, its old, dry timbers roaring like an inferno. Wood, apparently, would rather burn than melt.

"How was I supposed to know the place I remembered was right across the street from a portal?"

"Ex-portal," Leo said, his face pinched in the fire's glow. "Can anybody see C. K.?"

Piper leaned forward. The heat of the fire was so great it felt as if her skin was scorching. Through the smoke, Piper thought she could just make out a figure slumped in the gutter in front of the burning warehouse.

"There!" she said. "I think that's her!" As she spoke, the warehouse groaned. The roof caved inward, sending a flurry of sparks and a rush of flames straight up into the sky. Burning embers cascaded down onto the sidewalk. The figure in the gutter never moved.

"She's hurt!" Piper cried. Instinctively, she surged forward.

"Wait, Piper. Let me go!" Leo commanded, detaining her with a firm hand on her arm. "You two wait here," he said, his gaze shifting to encompass Paige. "Keep out of sight."

At that moment, Piper realized the air was filled with more than the sound of the flames. Above the fire's roar, she could hear the wail of sirens.

"Go, Leo," she urged.

He took off across the street at a dead run. Huddled together in the mouth of the alley, Piper and Paige watched him reach the crumpled figure, kneel, and lift it into his arms. Then he moved back across the street as quickly as he could.

The sirens were closer now. Another few minutes and the authorities would arrive.

C. K.'s face was deathly pale, her body completely limp in Leo's arms. There were red splotches on her where flying sparks had struck her face.

"Please tell me she's not dead," Paige breathed.

"She can't be dead," Piper answered shortly. "That thing controlling her still needs her alive. Orb straight back to the Manor," she instructed Leo. "See what you can do for her. Paige and I will wait for Phoebe."

"Just stay out of sight until you see her," Leo warned.

"Will do," Piper said.

Without further discussion, Leo orbed out. No sooner had the sparkling that always accompanied the orbing process ceased, than the Halliwell SUV roared around the far corner. The sirens were getting louder.

"Phoebe! Here!" Paige called.

At the sight of her sisters, Phoebe jerked to a stop, reaching to swing the back door open as she did so.

"Hurry! Get in!" she yelled.

Piper and Paige took the distance between the alley and the SUV at a dead run. Piper dove in first; Paige scrambled in right behind her. She shut the door with a clash of metal.

"Floor it!"

Phoebe gunned the SUV's powerful engine. The vehicle shot forward with a squeal of tires. She rounded the corner, the momentum carrying her for half a block. As soon as possible, she eased off the gas and slowed to the speed limit. There was no sense in attracting unwanted attention and being unsafe all at the same time.

"Everybody all right?" she asked after a moment, glancing into the rearview mirror.

"We're good," Paige confirmed. She sat up, pushing her hair out of her face and reaching for her seatbelt.

"C. K.?" Phoebe asked.

"Leo orbed her to the Manor," Piper said, following Paige's example.

The scream of a siren silenced the sisters as a fire truck passed them, moving full speed in the opposite lane.

"That was close," Phoebe observed after a moment.

"Too close," Piper commented. "And I hate feeling like we're running from the authorities."

"We *are* running from the authorities," Paige said. "But it's our only choice. Sticking around to be questioned isn't going to help anything. In fact, it would only confuse things, considering that the target right before this one was your club."

"I know that," Piper said. "It's just . . . I feel a little bad about Detective Anderson. He's working so hard on something he doesn't understand."

An aid car streaked by them, lights flashing, sirens wailing. It was followed by several police cars.

"Well, we can't explain things to him," Phoebe said. "But we can try to help him."

"Just get us home as quickly as you can, okay, Phoebes?"

Phoebe tightened her grip on the steering wheel.

"You got it."

Seventeen

"Well, if this isn't déjà vu all over again, I don't know what is," Cole said, his tone distinctly grumpy. "C. K.'s sleeping it off upstairs, and we're down here wondering what to do next."

"I was all set to vote for panicking, myself," Paige put in, trying to distract Cole from what was obviously a very foul mood. He'd been almost to Berkeley when he'd received Phoebe's call re-routing him to Halliwell Manor. As a result, he'd gotten stuck in the terrible-no-matter-what-time-of-day-it-is traffic on the Bay Bridge in both directions, coming and going.

"But I've been informed that it's counterproductive," Paige went on.

"Does this mean I can't kick something?"

"Just so long as it isn't one of us," Phoebe said as she came into the living room carrying a tray loaded with lunch sandwiches. Piper was right on her heels, carrying chips and beverages. No sooner had they set the food down on the coffee table than Leo appeared from upstairs.

"How is she?" Piper asked.

"Sleeping," Leo answered simply.

"Gee, now there's a surprise," Cole observed.

"Cole, honey, sweetheart," Phoebe said. She turned toward him, hands on her hips. "We're all very sorry you got stuck on the bridge. Twice. We get that you didn't exactly like it. What we *don't* get is how soon you'll get over yourself. In case you hadn't noticed, we're in a pretty serious situation here. Don't you think that ought to have the priority?"

"Great—make me look selfish and petty," Cole complained.

Phoebe's eyebrows rose. "Oh, do you need my help with that?"

"Okay, children. Break it up," Piper said. She snagged a roast beef sandwich from the tray and thrust it into Cole's hands. "You. Eat," she commanded. She handed Phoebe turkey. "You, too," she said. "We are all going to eat to keep up our strength and replenish our brain cells. Then we're going to figure out how to stop Malvolio De Vermis from carrying out his evil plan.

"I figure we've got until midnight tonight. That's when All Souls' Day officially begins. Somehow, I can't imagine Malvolio waiting any longer than he absolutely has to. Particularly considering he's already been waiting for several hundred years."

"Too bad he can't get stuck in traffic," Paige observed, as she popped the top on a soda can.

Even Cole had to laugh at that. Phoebe grinned and wrapped her arms around him. "So traffic has the ability to turn you back into a demon, huh?"

"Yeah, but I'm willing to take mass transit from now on, just for you," Cole said, his face at long last relaxing into a smile.

"That's so sweet. Doesn't everybody else think that's sweet?" Phoebe asked.

Paige rolled her eyes. "Keep that up and I'm not going to be able to keep a single bite down," she replied.

For a moment, the extended Halliwell clan replenished their brain cells in companionable silence.

Cole realized his apparent frustration about being stuck in traffic had actually been frustration over his seeming powerlessness. Even working together, the Charmed Ones and their partners hadn't been able to prevent the power of the *De Vermis Mysteriis* from striking once again. It had literally snatched C. K. right out from under Phoebe, Paige, and Piper's noses.

But at least we know we can turn to one another, rely on one another, to regroup and try again, Cole thought. It was one of the things that never ceased to astonish him, so different from life in the back-stabbing—often literally—demon realm. The ability to unite was one of the things that made the Charmed Ones what they were. And made them and those who loved and fought beside them strong.

Cole took a swig of soda, then set his can down on a coaster.

"Okay, so—now that I'm over myself, who wants to tell me what the plan is?" he inquired.

"Well, I should think that's pretty obvious," Paige said. "Stop Malvolio De Vermis from destroying the world as we know it."

"That's the goal," Cole countered. "What's the *plan*? How, exactly, do we intend to stop him?"

"We have to prevent any more portals from being destroyed, that's for sure," Phoebe put in.

"I agree," Cole nodded. "But it still leaves us with the same question, doesn't it? How do we go about it?"

"Do we even know where the other portals are, Leo?" Piper asked. "If we knew where they were, we could, I don't know, watch them or something."

"I don't know their exact locations," Leo admitted, his face slightly scrunched in concentration, his tone preoccupied. "But maybe you could scry for them."

"Okay, so we scry for the other portals," Piper said. "Maybe we'll get lucky and there'll only be one of them! That way, we'll know right where Malvolio has to strike."

"And where C. K. will have to be," Phoebe put in. "We need to keep as close an eye on her as

possible. We've certainly got plenty of unpleasan
evidence about what happens when we don't."

"Not to be the doomsday guy," Cole said
"But do we even know she's where she's sup
posed to be right now?"

"The only way out of Paige's room is down
the stairs or out a window," Piper reminded
"Besides, I don't think C. K.'s going to get ver
far in the shape she was in."

"That may not make much difference," Col
countered. "Malvolio De Vermis is going t
make sure his conduit is in position when h
needs it, where he needs it, no matter what kin
of shape she's in. Once he's successful and th
Ward is destroyed, C. K. will have served he
purpose. It won't matter if she doesn't survive."

"Look on the bright side much?" Phoeb
inquired.

"I was a DA. Everyone's guilty until prove
innocent in my book," Cole reminded.

"Speaking of C. K., what about her?" Paig
put in. "I mean, can we, you know, trust her?"

There was a silence.

"I think we can when she's herself," Pipe
answered finally. "The trouble is, she's no matc
for Malvolio De Vermis."

"She's not alone there," Cole snorted.

"Okay, focusing on what we can't accomplis
is really going to depress me," Phoebe sai
forcefully. "How about we focus on what we ca
do, instead?"

She began to tick off items one by one on her fingers.

"We can try to scry for the remaining portals. We can monitor C. K. as much as possible. It won't prevent Malvolio from using her again, but it will cut down on future nasty surprises."

"What about the Book of Shadows?" Paige inquired. "Now that we think we've identified the power behind the *De Vermis Mysteriis*, shouldn't we see if the Book of Shadows has anything to add?"

"I am so right there with you," Phoebe nodded. "Maybe the Book can find an angle we've overlooked."

"Sounds like a good to-do list," Piper commented. She rose from the couch, briskly. "Let's get on it. Paige, why don't you check on C. K., since she's back in your room. Leo and I can scry for the remaining portals. Cole, maybe you should check on the *De Vermis Mysteriis*. Make sure it's still where we think it is, but speaking of avoiding future nasty surprises . . ."

"Right," Cole nodded. "You know, I've been wondering—"

He never got to the end of his thought. A bloodcurdling scream from upstairs cut him off in midsentence.

Phoebe shot to her feet. "C. K.!" she called out.

Then, before Cole could stop her, she started for the stairs at a dead run.

Eighteen

"Phoebe! Wait! You don't know what's up there!"
Cole yelled. In a move that was purely instinc-
tive, he dashed after her. Catching up to her, he
pulled her back, flattening them both against the
wall. Before either could so much as blink, a second figure hurtled past.

"For crying out loud—I meant *nobody* knows
what's up there!" Cole cried. But by then Piper
was taking the stairs two at a time.

"C. K.! It's all right. We're coming," she
shouted.

"Piper, wait! Cole's right!" Phoebe called.

There was another terrified scream from the
second story. Then C. K.'s anguished voice. "No,
no! Get away from me!"

As if her words had produced a response
from whatever had so frightened her, there was
a shrieking, rending sound—like hundreds of
rusty nails being yanked out of wood all at

once. Paige clapped her hands over her ears, her eyes fixed on the landing just as Piper reached it.

"Piper! Look out!"

At the last possible moment, Piper skidded to a stop. Above her head, floating above the landing like a storm cloud, was a dark, sinewy shadow. For one split second as all eyes gazed upward, it seemed to reshape itself, flickering into what might have been a human form.

And then, coiling into itself like the serpent that was the crest of the family De Vermis, it launched itself forward, straight at Piper. In the same instant Piper instinctively shot out her hands to blow up the attacker, but it just kept coming at her, no worse for her magic.

Piper screamed as the shadow struck her full in the chest, *passing through her* and emerging on the other side. Her knees gave way and she tumbled to the landing, her face white and still.

"Piper!" Phoebe yelled. Side by side now, she and Cole rushed up the staircase, with Paige and Leo close behind.

Above them, the shadow gave a final shriek, then shot straight through the wall. In spite of the fact that he'd started out last, Leo reached Piper first.

"Piper," he said, easing her into a sitting position. Her head lolled against his chest, limp as a rag doll's.

Phoebe was just kneeling down, her fingers

desperately searching for a pulse when she heard C. K.'s voice cry out.

"Oh, my God! She's dead! She's dead and it's all my fault!"

Nineteen

"Piper is *not* dead!" Leo said forcefully.

He stood, gathering the still-unconscious Piper into his arms. Then he moved swiftly down the stairs, the others stepping aside to make way. He carried Piper to the living room and laid her gently on the couch. Almost at once Phoebe was beside him, pressing a blanket into his hands. Leo wrapped it around Piper. If she was in shock, it was important to keep her warm.

"I'll go get a glass of water," Phoebe offered.

"Let us do it," Paige put in swiftly. She stood at the entrance to the living room, her arm linked through one of C. K.'s in a gesture that served the dual purpose of offering comfort and keeping the other girl from running.

"Then we'll make tea," Paige went on. "That's what Piper always does in a crisis. It's only right someone should make it for her.

Come on, C. K. Let's go put the kettle on."

Her arm still linked through C. K.'s, Paige tugged her in the direction of the kitchen. A moment later, C. K. returned on her own, carrying a glass of water. It was only about half full. Her hand was shaking so badly water sloshed from side to side like a storm at sea.

"Just put it on the table close to Leo, please, C. K.," Phoebe said.

Moving slowly, as if fearing a sudden movement on her part might further endanger Piper, C. K. did as Phoebe instructed.

"How does he *know* she's all right?" she asked, her huge, frightened eyes fixed on Leo where he knelt beside Piper.

Leo's eyes were closed, and one hand grasped Piper's wrist as if gauging her pulse. Then with one gentle movement, Leo pressed his other hand, palm down, in the center of Piper's chest at the exact same spot the shadow had passed through it. A faint blush of color bloomed in Piper's cheeks.

"Omigod," C. K. whispered, her tone awed. "You guys have . . . powers, too, don't you?" Her eyes tracked around the room, taking in Phoebe and Cole. "All of you."

Phoebe made another split-second decision— the second one that day—and both involved revealing the fact that the Halliwells were special to people who were essentially total strangers.

"Yes, C. K., we do," she answered quietly.

C. K. fumbled for a chair and sat down abruptly, as if her legs simply refused to hold her. Tears streamed down her cheeks. She didn't seem to notice.

"She's going to be okay, C. K.," Phoebe said again.

"I believe you," C. K. responded. "It's just . . . this is going to sound so stupid and selfish at a time like this, but . . . I'm so glad you guys have powers! All my life, I worried there was something wrong with me. I felt so alone."

"There's nothing wrong with you, and you aren't alone. You never were," Piper said in a weak and raspy voice.

"Piper!" C. K. cried, springing to her feet.

"In the flesh," Piper said as she pushed herself upright. "Ooof," she went on, rubbing her chest with the heel of one hand. "Make that the bruised and aching flesh." Her eyes found Leo's, and she lifted a loving hand to his face. "Hi."

"Hi, yourself," Leo said with a smile. "Welcome back."

"Glad to be back," Piper answered.

There was a rattle of crockery as Paige returned carrying a tray laden with cups and saucers.

"Tea, anyone?"

"Okay, so," Paige said several moments later. She'd just finished pouring tea and handing it around. She'd brought some cookies out too.

"You really want me to gain five pounds, don't you?" Phoebe muttered as Paige passed her the plate. "Wait a minute, I know. You're lusting after that new red dress I just brought home."

"Well, you have to admit," Paige remarked, smirking, as in spite of her words Phoebe snatched two cookies from the plate, "red *is* my color."

"And it looks so nice with both black and blue," Phoebe commented. "Get those things away from me before I take a poke at you."

"Cookie, Cole?" Paige inquired sweetly.

C. K. gaped at the makeshift tea party. "I just don't get it," she confessed. "Something totally weird and spooky just happened. How can you guys act so . . . normal?"

"How else should we act?" Piper asked matter-of-factly. "We *are* normal. And so are you. Just think of this as recharging the batteries before we tackle the next crisis."

"Speaking of which," Paige put in. "I hate to be the one to end the fun and games, but what *was* that thing that attacked Piper? A ghost?"

"Welll," Phoebe said, drawing out the word. She took a sip of tea, as if using the time to assemble her thoughts. "I suppose a ghost would be the most obvious suspect. Bringing her fiancé back from the dead was C. K.'s intention when she performed that spell."

"No way," C. K. put in firmly, shaking her head from side to side.

"No way, what, C. K.?" Piper inquired.

"No way would Jace try to scare or hurt either you or me. He just wasn't like that . . . when he was alive. People don't change who they are just because they're dead, do they?" She looked around the circle of faces. *"Do they?"*

"Under ordinary circumstances, no, they don't," Paige responded. "But I do think we have to take the un-ordinariness of these circumstances into some consideration. The book you used to cast the spell does contain some pretty majorly bad mojo."

"It didn't start out that way," Phoebe objected.

"True," Paige granted. "But even so. . . . Then there's the fact that Jace's death was sudden and accidental. No matter how wonderful he was in life, that combination often ends up spelling a soul in torment."

"Yes, but," Phoebe said.

"I don't think it was a ghost," Piper interrupted, effectively putting an end to her sisters' discussion. "It didn't look like one and it didn't feel like one."

"The first point is definitely true," Cole concurred. "Ghosts usually look like themselves, not like some movie-maker's special effect."

"Can you tell us what it felt like?" Leo inquired.

"It felt like . . ." Piper paused, her brow wrinkling in concentration, the heel of one hand absently rubbing the place on her chest through which the entity had passed.

"It felt like energy," she finally said.

"Energy?" Phoebe exclaimed.

Piper nodded. "That's the best way I can describe it. Psychic energy, all of the painful variety. That's what I felt when it passed through me. Pain and grief almost too great to bear."

"That might explain its form," Paige said thoughtfully. "It can't appear as human, because it isn't. Not completely. It's only certain aspects. Specifically, dark and painful ones."

"I'm thinking that's it, exactly," Piper nodded. She shot a quick glance at C. K. before she continued. "Lots of people probably wish they could separate themselves from their pain and grief. The person who created that entity actually managed to do it."

"You mean me, don't you?" C. K. said, her voice bitter. "You think whatever's going on—all the bad stuff you mentioned before—you think it's all my fault."

"No, I don't think it's all your fault, C. K.," Piper answered with quiet conviction. "But I also don't think there's any doubt about the fact that you *are* tied to what's going on."

"What *is* going on?" C. K. asked. "I want you to tell me. Really, I do. You just said I'm tied to it. Don't you think I have a right to know?"

"She's right," Phoebe put in. "Besides, there's not much point in keeping her in the dark. Maybe if she knows what she's up against, she can help fight it."

"Just make the explanation fast," Cole recommended. "We haven't got a lot of time."

"Essentially, what's going on is this," Piper said. "The book you used to cast your spell, the *De Vermis Mysteriis*, has the equivalent of an evil wizard trapped inside it. When you performed the spell, you accidentally made yourself a conduit for his power."

"Specifically," Phoebe went on, "he's using you to destroy various locations around the Bay Area that help keep the energy barrier between the realms of the living and the dead operating the way it should. They're known as portals. If enough portals are destroyed, the barrier will fail and we'll essentially be looking at the end of the world as we know it."

C. K. blinked rapidly, as if trying to take it all in. "Okay, so," she said after a moment, "you know a minute ago where I said I wanted you to tell me what was going on?

"I'm thinking I just changed my mind."

"So what do we do?" C. K. asked several moments later. "How do we stop what's going on?"

"I'm right with you there," Phoebe said. "But

to answer your question, we're not sure how. Not yet anyway."

C. K. took a breath. "Maybe I—I mean it might be better if—" She shook her head as if exasperated that she couldn't get the words out. "Do you guys want me to just go? Seems like you'd all be a lot safer if I wasn't around."

"Actually," Cole put in, "to tell you the truth, we're all a lot safer when you're right here where we can keep an eye on you."

"You don't trust me," C. K. said. Her face was flushed, but she met Cole's eyes steadily.

"We trust you, C. K.," Phoebe replied. "We *know for a fact* that what's going on is not your fault. But we also know your attempt to bring Jace back opened the door to some very powerful black magic that's using you to do its dirty work. When you're in its grip, you're part of the problem. There's just no way around that. I'm sorry."

"Okay, stand back, everybody," Piper suddenly put in. "I am just about to have a brainstorm. What if it makes her part of the solution, too?"

"How?" Paige inquired.

In response, Piper stood up.

"I say we go find out. Book of Shadows. Attic. Now. On the double."

Twenty

"You're sure about this?" Cole asked as they climbed the stairs. Piper and C. K. were in the lead, with Paige and Leo right behind them. Phoebe and Cole were bringing up the rear.

"Consulting the Book of Shadows is on the to-do list," Piper reminded.

Cole snorted. "That's not what I meant, and you know it, Piper. I'm not trying to say you're wrong. I'm just pointing out that this is a pretty big step you're about to take, one you haven't made with just anyone."

"He has a point, Piper," Phoebe supported. "And I'm not just saying that because, you know."

"All right then, yes, I am sure," Piper responded, as she opened the attic door. She escorted C. K. through, waited for Paige and Leo, then turned to face Phoebe and Cole. "She's part of the problem. We've established that. But if my hunch is right, she's part of the solution, too. Having her with us when we consult the Book of Shadows is the best way to find that out."

"You never said anything about a hunch," Phoebe protested. "All you said was brainstorm."

"I'm saying hunch now," Piper said.

"Oh well, that's different then," Phoebe acknowledged. She gestured. "Lead on."

Together they entered the attic. Cole shut the door. As one unit, the assembled group turned to face the Book of Shadows.

"Is that what I think it is?" C. K. inquired.

Piper nodded. "It's a book of spells. Specifically, a book of spells designed to help Phoebe, Paige, and I carry out our destiny: to protect the innocent."

C. K.'s expression brightened. "So, the spells in that book will make everything better, right?"

"That's not the way it works, C. K.," Phoebe said. "Making things better is a thing we have to do ourselves. Magic is a tool. A powerful one. But it doesn't replace the things you have to do on your own. Say, for instance, figuring out the difference between right and wrong."

"Congratulations," Paige put in. "You've just been given the Cliff's Notes version of the opening lecture in Magic 101."

"Phoebe's point," Piper spoke up firmly, "is that magic can't be viewed as a cure for all our problems. It can't be used to solve things we should be solving on our own. But that's exactly what you tried to do when you cast the spell to bring Jace back. You tried to substitute magic for your own healing process."

"But I didn't bring him back," C. K. protested.

"No, you didn't," Piper agreed. "But I think this afternoon's experiences have proved that you definitely summoned something. If my hunch is correct, figuring out what you—we—are supposed to do about it will put an end to it too."

Piper moved to stand before the Book of Shadows, gesturing for C. K. to accompany her. "Don't be afraid," she said. "This book is nothing like the one you used before. Just stand beside me and hold your hands out over the book. Palms down. Like this."

She demonstrated. Plainly nervous, C. K. did as Piper instructed, holding out her hands alongside Piper's. For a moment nothing happened. Then, the heavy cover of the Book of Shadows flipped back. One page turned. Then another, and another. Before long, they were moving so swiftly their passage was nothing but a blur. Above the book, C. K.'s hands began to tremble.

"Piper?"

"Just stay still," Piper said. "Don't worry. There's nothing to be afraid of."

As if their words had been some secret signal,

the pages stopped with one poised, upright. For a moment it wavered, floating first this way, then that, as if trying to make up its mind about something. Slowly, gently, Piper withdrew her hands so that only C. K.'s remained above the Book of Shadows. With a sigh, the page fluttered down into place. The book lay still.

"Okay, gather round, everybody," Piper said. "Let's see what the book can tell us."

Silence filled the attic as six pairs of eyes solemnly regarded the Book of Shadows.

"Oh, man," Paige said. "This is majorly weird. That's . . ."

"The same spell I used to try and bring Jace back from the dead," C. K. whispered. "A Spell to Restore a Riven Heart. What on earth is it doing here? I thought you said this book was a good thing."

"It is. And so was the *De Vermis Mysteriis*, in the beginning," Piper reminded her. "Actually, having a spell to restore something in the De Vermis makes perfect sense. That was Mileager De Vermis's original intention when he created it. To collect spells to heal, to restore."

"So what's it doing in the Book of Shadows?" Cole asked.

"I think it's a reminder," Piper answered, her tone thoughtful.

"To return to the original spell as a solution to our current crisis," Phoebe suggested.

"That's right," Piper nodded.

"Look, the illustrations are different," Paige said. She leaned over Piper's shoulder to point.

"I see that," Piper said. "This one," she pointed to a drawing of two figures, arms clasped tightly around one another, "accompanied the original spell. But in the original, you couldn't see their faces. You can now."

"That's my face," C. K. said. "I'm in your book." She put her hands to her cheeks as if they'd suddenly grown warm. "This is so freaky. I don't know whether to be terrified or honored."

"Try both," Phoebe commented. But she reached to pat C. K. on the shoulder.

"Okay," Piper said. "Everybody ready to hear my hunch? C. K. *did* summon something with her spell, just not what she intended to summon. You said yourself you hadn't been able to grieve for Jace, C. K. As if your feelings were somehow separate from you."

"Pain and grief," C. K. made the connection. "That's what you said you felt when that shadow-thing attacked you. You think it's *my* pain and grief, don't you? You think that's what I summoned."

"I do," Piper nodded. "I don't think it's Jace's actual death that's responsible for your pain, C. K., though of course Jace's death was a terrible blow for you. I think the true problem is that you haven't been able to mourn for him.

That's what's splitting your heart in two.

"When you pronounced a spell to restore your heart, the healing power that was the original intention of the De Vermis responded. It sent your grief to you."

"That's some hunch," Cole remarked.

"It gets better," Piper commented. "We've been dealing with the De Vermis as if it's completely evil. But look at the second illustration in the Book of Shadows."

Again she pointed, this time at an illustration of two identical figures, arm in arm. The figures were male, very definitely *not* C. K.

"That's new. We haven't seen that one before," said Cole.

"Actually, some of us have," Paige corrected. "That's one of the two illustrations of the De Vermis brothers that was in the book Gibson, the proprietor of the Seeking Eye, showed us. It was a journal written by Mileager De Vermis, the good guy."

"Is he the one on the right, or the one on the left?" Cole muttered under his breath.

Phoebe poked him in the ribs. "Very funny. But just in case anybody *else* is interested, I'm starting to get a hunch of my own. This is all about *restoration*, isn't it? That's why the Book of Shadows wants us to focus on the original spell."

"Great minds work alike," Piper said. She regarded Phoebe with a triumphant smile.

Paige snorted. "And, apparently, some minds are just plain slow. I still don't get what you're trying to say."

"Boy, am I glad you said that first," C. K. murmured, sotto voce.

"Mind if I take a crack at explaining?" Phoebe asked.

"Be my guest," said Piper.

Phoebe pulled in a deep breath.

"Okay, so . . . we consult the Book of Shadows looking for answers about how to stop Malvolio De Vermis from destroying the world. The book refers us to C. K.'s spell. It also shows us two examples of restoration at work. C. K. and herself, her grief, which is what her original casting of the spell summoned, and the De Vermis brothers themselves. Those are the things that have to be made whole, restored to one another, before the evil can be stopped."

She exhaled and turned to Piper. "How'd I do?"

"I'd say you got it in a nutshell."

"You're saying I have to embrace my own grief?" C. K. said. "I have to carry all that dark stuff around inside me all the time?"

"Not forever, C. K.," Piper said quietly. "But you do have to work through your own grief, your own pain. It's one of those things magic can't do for you."

"We all have to do it," Paige put in. "It's part of being human."

"But . . . I'm afraid," C. K. confessed.

Piper reached to give her hand a squeeze. "That's perfectly normal. And, to tell you the truth, I think it's pretty healthy. Healthy people don't deliberately seek out pain, C. K. But sometimes they do recognize that they have to go through it to get where they're going. It's part of how we grow. It isn't easy, but it's necessary. You'll get through it. Trust me on this one. I should know."

C. K.'s eyes widened in sudden understanding. "You lost someone, too," she said.

"I did," Piper acknowledged. "Let's just say I didn't take it very well. That's how I know you've got to come to terms with your own grief all on your own. You've got to be strong."

C. K. lifted her chin as if accepting a challenge. "Okay, let's say I manage to do that," she said. "Then what?"

"My question exactly," Paige said. Silently, she placed her hands on Phoebe and Piper's shoulders, linking the three sisters together. Showing her support for Piper and Phoebe's memories of the sister who was gone.

"Look at the illustrations again," Piper instructed.

"That doesn't exactly help, Piper," Cole said, his tone reflecting his growing impatience. "The De Vermis brothers have their arms linked together like they're best buddies. How likely is that?"

"Not very," Piper acknowledged. "But that doesn't mean their coming together isn't what's required, Cole. I'd say the Book of Shadows makes what has to happen for Malvolio De Vermis to be defeated quite clear. That which had been torn apart must be restored. That means the brothers must at least be reunited— occupy the same plane."

"Well at least we know where Malvolio is," Phoebe said. "He's trapped inside the *De Vermis Mysteriis*, put there by his big brother. But what about Mileager? Nobody knows what happened to him, do they? We don't even know if he's still alive."

"Yes, we do," Leo spoke up for the first time. He'd remained silent throughout the Book of Shadows consult, standing aside from the others. Now, they all swung around to face him.

"We do? Since when?" Piper asked, her tone astonished.

"Since I followed up your hunch with one of my own," Leo replied. "I think Mileager De Vermis's whereabouts is the thing the Council of Elders is hiding."

Twenty-one

"Oh, man," Paige said. "I am *seriously* not certain I want to hear this."

"You can join the club on that one," Phoebe told her. "Okay, Leo. Tell us what you mean."

"Just what I said," Leo answered. "I think the location of Mileager De Vermis is the thing the Elders have been keeping from us. You remember I had the sense that they were holding back something."

"Of course we remember," Piper said. "But why do you think it has to do with Mileager?"

"For years there have been rumors of a powerful mage," Leo answered. "Actually, it's more specific than rumors. More like a folktale or a really good bedtime story. According to the tale, the mage is being provided with a safe haven—sort of like he's in protective custody. The Elders protect the mage's location and identity, because, if they're revealed at the wrong time, the fate of the world could hang in the balance.

"I never paid much attention to it, to tell you the truth. The Over-world is filled with stories. It's hard to separate fact from legend. But this one has been around a long time—for centuries, in fact."

"That timeframe would be long enough to accommodate the De Vermis brothers," Paige commented.

"Wait a minute," C. K. said. "Who are the Elders? What's a—"

Piper put a quieting hand on her shoulder. "When this is all over, we'll explain everything, we promise. Right now it's important that you let Leo finish."

"Okay, if you say so," C. K. said, subsiding.

"So you think the mage in the story is Mileager," Phoebe said. "I have to admit, I'm pretty much right behind you. Gibson, the owner of the Seeking Eye, said Mileager vanished at the same moment Malvolio became imprisoned in the *De Vermis Mysteriis*. Mileager's whereabouts have been a mystery ever since. No pun intended."

"None taken," Leo replied.

"I still don't see why," Cole began.

"Because there's more," Leo interrupted. "The story is very specific about one thing: When the time is right, the mage will be revealed. Not only that, *he will be restored unto himself.* Only then will the world be made secure."

"Oh, man," Piper said. "There's that restore thing again."

Leo nodded. "That's pretty much what I thought. That's what finally made me remember the story, in fact."

"I gotta admit, it does add up," Cole agreed. "But why wouldn't the Elders just tell you about Mileager and ask you to sit tight?"

"Please," Piper said before Leo could answer. "Think about who you're talking about."

"Right. Sorry," Cole said. "So I assume asking them *now* is out?"

"I think so," Leo answered slowly. "The legend does make clear that the timing of the mage's reappearance is incredibly important. Assuming that the mage in the tale really is Mileager de Vermis, I don't think the Elders will be willing to reveal his location until they think the time is right."

"But what if *their* timing is off?" Piper asked quietly, concern in her voice. "Isn't *when the time is right* something Mileager should be deciding for himself?"

"I'm inclined to agree with you," Leo said, his expression solemn. "At the very least, I'd say Mileager ought to be informed about what's going on. The trouble with the legend is that it's a little short on details. It's hard to know just what *safe haven* means. Mileager De

Vermis may already know what's going on. I don't think the Elders would deliberately keep things from him. But if keeping him safe means he's cut off . . ."

"Then when the time was right for him to be *restored unto himself*, he'd be completely unprepared," Phoebe filled in. "A thing which would definitely *not* be to the world's advantage. I think it's safe to assume bad-boy Malvolio will hardly be thrilled at the prospect of a family reunion, unless it's to exact some sort of revenge. Being trapped in that book has not exactly made him a happy camper."

"Right on all counts, Phoebe," Leo said. "That's why I'm thinking of trying something."

"A non-Elders-sanctioned thing?" Piper inquired.

"A non-Elders-sanctioned thing," Leo said.

Piper pulled in a deep breath, then expelled it. "What do you have in mind?" she asked.

"There's a special orbing technique," Leo explained. "It isn't used all that often, mostly because it isn't necessary. Usually, when I orb, I have some sense of the physical details of the place where I'm going."

"What's orbing?" C. K. suddenly blurted out. Then she held up both hands as if in a stick-up. "I know—when all this is over, C. K. Sorry, I just couldn't seem to help myself."

A swift smile illuminated Leo's serious face. "Don't worry about it."

"The special orbing technique, Leo?" Paige prompted.

"It has to do with focusing on an individual, rather than a place," Leo went on. "Sort of like the reverse of what Paige does when she object-summons. In this case, I'd let the person I'm focusing on draw me to him."

"Okay, time out," Phoebe said. "Does nobody else see a problem? Mileager and Malvolio De Vermis are twins, Leo. *Identical twins.* How can you be sure won't focus on Mileager and end up with Malvolio?"

"He can't," Cole spoke up suddenly, stepping to Leo's side. "That's why both of us are going."

Twenty-two

"What?" Phoebe and Leo cried simultaneously.

"It makes sense, Leo," Cole insisted. "You're not a hundred percent certain what you'll find even if you end up in the right place. There's no way you should go in without a backup. I'm thinking I'm your best bet."

"He has a point," Paige put in quietly.

"I hate it when that happens," Phoebe said.

"I'm not exactly wild about the scenario myself," Piper spoke up. "But I agree with Leo that we have to try something. There are enough wild cards flying around here already. I don't think we can run the risk of leaving Mileager De Vermis uninformed."

"So, we're agreed, then," Leo said. "Cole and I will attempt to orb to Mileager's location. After that, I think we just have to play it by ear."

"Agreed," Piper nodded. "Meanwhile, we'll

scry for the other portals, see if we can come up with a way to protect them."

"That sounds good," Leo said. He and Piper embraced, as did Phoebe and Cole. Paige and C. K. stood side by side, watching the couples with concerned eyes. Paige had one arm around C. K.'s shoulders, including her in the group.

"Be careful, please," Piper whispered.

"I'm always careful," Leo replied. "We'll be back as soon as we can."

"Take care of yourself," Phoebe cautioned.

"Where's the fun in that?" Cole replied. But he leaned down to give her a swift, hard kiss. "Back before you know it."

The four women linked arms for a united send-off. Leo stepped to the Book of Shadows, his eyes fixed on the illustration of the twins.

"Ready?" inquired Cole.

"As I'll ever be," Leo said.

Cole stepped up beside him and placed a hand on Leo's shoulder. Leo took a breath, and closed his eyes. For a moment, the image of what Phoebe sincerely hoped was Mileager De Vermis almost seemed to hover in the air, so great was Leo's concentration. Then, in a shower of bright blue sparks, Leo and Cole orbed out.

"Whoa—beam me up, Scotty," C. K. said, after a moment. "So that's orbing, huh?"

"That's orbing," Piper nodded.

All of a sudden, C. K. grinned. "Looks pretty

cool," she said. "You think, someday when this is all over, I'll get to try it?"

"Actually, you already have," Paige said. "You just weren't exactly conscious at the time."

"Oh, man!" C. K. exclaimed. "Bummer."

"Okay, everybody, enough chat," Phoebe proclaimed. "We've got work of our own to do. Let's go see if we can find the remaining portals."

Half an hour later, Piper pushed back from the dining room table, and rubbed a hand across her tired eyes. In front of her was the map of the Bay Area she and Phoebe had used while performing the scrying spell. Push pins marked the portal locations they'd discovered.

Piper regarded the colorful pins somberly.

"Is this what they mean when they say be careful what you ask for?"

"You can say that again," Paige said.

"I could," Piper admitted. "But I won't. I'm too tired. Scrying always seriously takes it out of me."

"C. K.'s making more tea," Phoebe informed her. She reached over to give Piper's arm a quick pat.

Piper smiled. Then turned her attention to the push pins.

"I hate to say this, but San Francisco, we have very definitely got a problem."

Six of them, to be precise.

One more location than the team could cover

if they split up, even if they included Leo and
Cole. Not only that, splitting up just might create
more problems than it solved. It would eliminate
the possibility of the sisters using their powers
in concert as the Charmed Ones.

"What now?" Paige asked somberly. "There's
no way we can protect all six portals at once.
And no way we can know which one will be the
target. What are we supposed to do, draw
straws?"

"Use me," C. K.'s voice said. She came into
the dining room, carrying the teapot on its tray.
She set it on the table, then sat down beside
Paige, facing Phoebe and Piper.

"What did you just say?" Phoebe inquired.

"Use me," C. K. said again. "It's the obvious
choice. Every single time something bad has
happened, I've been there, haven't I? In fact, if
I'm getting what's going on, the bad guy—
Malvolio—*needs* me to be there. He can't do his
stuff without me, right?"

"Right," Piper acknowledged.

"So, if he can use me, why can't you?" C. K.
asked. "Don't worry about trying to figure out
which portal he's going to attack ahead of
time. Just stick with me and I'll lead you right
to it. Then all you have to do is stop me in
time."

"Oh, gee, is that all?" Paige rolled her eyes.
But she gave C. K.'s shoulders a quick squeeze
to show her appreciation. "I hate to think of us

using you just like the bad guy, but I have to admit, it's the best plan I've heard."

"But you wouldn't be using me like the bad guy," C. K. countered, her tone earnest. She leaned forward, her eyes moving between the three sisters as she tried to get her point across.

"You'd be using me to *get* to him. To stop him. That's not the same thing at all. You guys—you *see* me. You accept me, all of me. Nobody's done that since Jace died. And even he couldn't do it the way you can. Because you understand . . . about the powers.

"Upstairs just now, Piper said I was more than just a part of the problem. I was part of the solution, too. Let me prove it. Let me help."

The Charmed Ones had a silent communication moment. Then Piper reached for C. K.'s hand across the table.

"Okay, C. K.," she said. "But we do this our way."

Twenty-three

"I don't suppose you have any idea where we are."

"You wouldn't settle for 'not in San Francisco anymore,' would you?" Leo asked.

Cole snorted.

"I didn't think so," Leo said. Hands on his hips, he looked around.

Leo's attempts to orb himself and Cole to Mileager De Vermis's safe haven had transported them to what appeared to be end of a long tunnel made entirely of glass. The space in which Leo and Cole now stood was flooded with cool, bright light. So bright it made Leo wish he'd brought along a pair of sunglasses. The light was so dazzling it was difficult to see anything else.

Specifically, it was difficult to tell how much longer the tunnel extended or even where it led.

At least it did seem clear that he hadn't orbed

the two of them between the covers of the *De Vermis Mysteriis*, which definitely had to be considered a plus. Now the only question was, was Mileager De Vermis anywhere nearby, and, if so, how far away was he?

There was only one way to find out. Directly behind where Cole and Leo stood, the tunnel . . . ended. It wasn't sealed; it just sort of seemed to stop. They'd discovered that when Cole had accidentally taken one too many steps backward. Only Leo's quick action had prevented him from falling out.

"Well, at least we know which direction to go," he remarked.

"Just like a Whitelighter. Always making the decisions for everyone," Cole came back. But his grin told Leo he was grateful for the action, and glad to be along.

"You're enjoying this, aren't you?" Leo said. "I'm not so sure you're supposed to be doing that. This is serious business, don't forget."

"Hey—I can be serious and appreciate a good adventure all at the same time," Cole said. "I think they call that multi-tasking." He gave Leo a brisk slap on the back. "Lead on."

"Oh, thanks a lot," Leo said.

"Hey—I'm the backup man, remember? That means you go first."

Leo tentatively took one step forward, then another, testing his weight. Although it was clear, the floor of the tunnel proved quite sturdy.

"Seems secure enough," he said. He began to move along the tunnel at a brisk pace, Cole right on his heels.

"Let's just hope whatever this is made of will support your ego."

Cole had to chuckle. Leo was finally developing a sense of humor.

"How long have we been doing this?" Cole asked a few moments later.

"Haven't the faintest idea," Leo answered.

Since starting out, their progression along the tunnel had been determined and steady. Unfortunately, it also seemed to be getting them absolutely nowhere. No matter how far along Cole and Leo walked, the end of the tunnel stayed immediately at their backs, almost as if it were vanishing behind them as they moved along it.

"Maybe it's some sort of test," Cole said. "Keep at it long enough, we'll prove ourselves worthy of talking to the mage, or something like that."

"Maybe," Leo said. "Though the Elders wouldn't really have had a reason to set up anything like that. I don't think they expected anyone to ever get this far."

"Assuming we're in the right place," Cole said.

"For a backup man, you sure are pessimistic."

"I'm *realistic*," Cole said. "I mean, let's face it.

So far we haven't seen anything to make us believe we're anywhere near this Mileager De Vermis guy."

"It's about time," a new voice said. "All you had to do was say my name, you know."

Leo stopped so abruptly Cole crashed right into him. The two came to a dead stop in the tunnel, staring straight ahead.

In front of them stood a young man dressed in the elaborate clothing of Renaissance Italy. He wore a doublet and hose. His feet were encased in soft leather boots. A short cape hung from his shoulders. The symbol embossed on the cover of the *De Vermis Mysteriis*, two serpents twined together, dangled from a heavy silver chain around his neck. He bowed low, then straightened.

"Please pardon me if I sounded rude. But you're my first visitors in almost five hundred years," Mileager De Vermis said.

"So that's how long you've been here? Five hundred years?" Cole asked.

"Give or take," Mileager De Vermis replied.

He, Cole, and Leo were now seated in what Leo could only assume was Mileager's main living area. Though it was made of the same material as the tunnel, the light was less piercing here, due mostly to the fact that the chamber was adorned with the opulent furnishings of Mileager's original time.

Rugs covered the floor. Tapestries adorned the walls, though Cole still hadn't figured out how they stayed up. The three men sat facing one another across a large trestle table, Leo and Cole on one side, Mileager De Vermis on the other. He'd offered them refreshments. They'd declined.

"You were quite right to assume I was the mage to whom the Elders gave their protection," Mileager said now with a glance at Leo. "That was very well done, even if you did defy them by coming here. You could be in quite a lot of trouble, you know."

"Thanks, I think," Leo said. "And, yes, I know."

Mileager De Vermis laughed, then quickly sobered. "I'm sorry. I know my behavior must seem odd. Allow me to assure you that I *am* in my right mind. But you have no idea what it's like not to have anyone to talk to for five hundred years. The Elders, though well intentioned, hardly count. I probably don't have to tell you that they're really pretty stuffy."

Leo's lips twitched as if he was fighting a smile. Cole stifled a chuckle.

"Ah, so you do understand," Mileager said.

"Well," Cole admitted, with a gesture in Leo's direction. "He does more than I do."

"Of course. That would make sense," Mileager nodded. "I imagine your masters, or perhaps I should say *former* masters, were a good deal more exciting."

There was a startled silence.

"You know about me . . . about us?" Cole asked.

"But of course," Mileager De Vermis replied. "I've been kept safe, not in the dark. In fact, I'm aware of a great deal of what goes on in the world. And I'm certainly aware of the fact that it's presently in a great deal of trouble, some of which could be considered my fault."

"So you'll help us, then," Leo said.

"Certainly," Mileager answered. "When it's time. The tales about me aren't just fancy legends. There's a reason they're told the way they are. I cannot leave this haven, cannot intervene in any way, until the time is right. Until the right circumstances arise. If I try to intervene before, I'll only help to bring about the very thing we're hoping to avoid."

"The end of the world," Leo murmured.

"Just so," Mileager nodded.

"But *how* will you intervene?" Cole asked.

At Cole's question, a shadow passed over Mileager De Vermis's face. For the first time, Cole noticed that, although the mage was still youthful in appearance, the areas around his eyes and mouth were etched with fine lines of sorrow. The Elders might have been able to keep Mileager safe from evil, but that wasn't the same as keeping him safe from pain.

"I will do the thing I've both longed for and dreaded for five hundred years," Mileager answered quietly. "I will be reunited with my brother."

As if the mention of his brother had made him restless, Mileager De Vermis rose and began to pace around the room.

"How shall I explain about Malvolio?" he said after a moment. "I guess the simplest way would be to say that he was jealous of me from the moment of our births. Literally. It's absurd, of course. As if I had anything to do with the order in which we were born.

"But I am the elder. That cannot be denied, just as it cannot be denied that, in the time into which we were born, this made a great difference in virtually all aspects of our lives. I was the one who was favored as we grew up. I would inherit my father's wealth and lands, Malvolio would not.

"My brother and I were close in many ways. We forgave each other many things as we grew from boys into men. But my having been born first was the one thing Malvolio could never forgive. In time, it destroyed his love for me. It has been my life's work to resist letting it destroy my love for him."

"The *De Vermis Mysteriis*," Cole suddenly said.

Mileager De Vermis swung toward him, his eyes widening. "That's very perceptive of you," he said after a moment. "And, if you don't mind my saying so, somewhat surprising. I'd have thought your companion"—he gestured to Leo—"would have been the first one to figure that out, given his background."

"He may have," Cole answered honestly. "It's just that he's the strong, silent type, while I tend to speak my mind."

"You should," Mileager said simply. "It's a good one. And yes, your surmise is correct. I did begin the *De Vermis Mysteriis* in the hope that collecting spells for balance, for healing and restoration, would help me find a way to be reconciled with my brother. It didn't exactly work, obviously."

"And when he tried to turn the good you'd created into evil, you imprisoned him inside it," Leo filled in quietly. "You probably hoped that would accomplish something, too. Other than keeping him confined."

"Of course I did," Mileager nodded. "I hoped it might heal him, given enough time. Yet another way in which I've failed."

"You know what they say," Cole put in. "Third time's the charm."

"I sincerely hope so," Mileager De Vermis said. "Because I don't think I'll survive to try a fourth time."

"But you are determined to stop him this time, right?" Cole said. "You won't get all brotherly and sentimental at the last minute and wimp out? You do understand what's at stake if we lose?"

"I understand," Mileager answered. "And, although I am unfamiliar with the term you use, I can assure you that I will not shirk my duty. I will do what must be done to stop Malvolio. But you cannot expect me to do it gladly. No matter what he does, he will always be my brother."

"Okay," Cole said, rising to his feet. "I'm sold." He turned to Leo. "I say we get back to the Manor and let the girls know we can count on Mileager's help—at the right time, of course. Till then, we'll do the best we can on our own."

"Sounds good," Leo agreed. He, too, rose to his feet and moved to shake Mileager De Vermis's hand. "Thank you for your hospitality."

"Oh, but I thought you understood," Mileager said. A spasm of concern and confusion passed across his face.

Leo stopped dead in his tracks. Cole sucked in an audible breath.

"Why do I think I'm not going to like this?" he said.

"Understand what?" Leo inquired.

"The way this place,"—Mileager waved a hand to indicate the room around them—"the haven, functions. There are reasons the Elders sought to keep my location a secret, not all of them for my protection. Many were for the protection of the curious as well.

"Once you entered this place, you became bound by its laws in precisely the same way that

I am bound by them. You cannot leave here until I do. Until the time is right."

"You're saying we're trapped here," Cole said.

Unexpectedly, Mileager De Vermis's face brightened. "I have just realized the meaning of a response which has always intrigued me," he confessed.

"And what would that be, exactly?" Cole asked.

As quickly as it had brightened, Mileager's expression sobered.

"I believe it goes: You got it in one."

Twenty-four

"Something has got to be seriously wrong," Piper said. "Where are they? They should have been back hours ago."

"Make that trip one more time and you'll wear a hole through the carpet," Phoebe remarked, her tone tense as she watched Piper move back and forth across the living room yet again.

"So I pace when I'm nervous," Piper said. "When did that become a crime?" She glared at Phoebe, huddled in one of the living room's overstuffed chairs. "It's better than just sitting around."

"I'm conserving energy," Phoebe protested.

"Ha!" Piper exclaimed as she spun on one heel and made her way back across the room.

"Glad to see at least she changed locations," Paige said as she entered the room.

Before pacing in the living room, Piper had

paced in the kitchen. Then she'd paced in the dining room after giving up on choking down more than a few bites of the take-out Chinese they'd ordered to keep their strength up. For once in her life, Piper hadn't offered to cook, and for this, Phoebe had been grateful. Piper was so preoccupied, chances were pretty good she'd have left something on the stove and burned the place down.

But nothing could take their minds off of the truth: Cole and Leo had been gone for hours. Gone too long. And every second that ticked past brought the Charmed Ones closer to midnight. Closer to a confrontation with an evil out to destroy everything they loved.

For a moment Phoebe took her eyes off Piper to sneak a glance at C. K., sitting opposite her on the couch. She'd been quiet and withdrawn all evening, but then Phoebe had to figure she had a right to be pretty tense herself.

"Will you please stop doing that, Phoebe?" C. K. demanded, suddenly coming to life.

"Doing what?" Phoebe asked, sitting up a little straighter in her chair. *Was this it?* she wondered. Was Malvolio De Vermis starting to take C. K. over?

"You know what," C. K. came back, her tone cross. "All evening you've been watching me as if you expected me to do the Linda Blair thing at any moment."

"Linda Blair thing? What Linda Blair thing?" Paige spoke up.

"You know, that thing from the *Exorcist*," C. K. said, "where her head turns all the way around. Phoebe's been watching me all night, waiting to see if I'll perform any tricks when the evil takes over. For the record, I'm getting pretty tired of it."

"I know we're all feeling a little strained," Paige began.

"No projectile vomiting," Phoebe interrupted.

Halfway across the living room, Piper stopped dead in her tracks.

"*What?*"

"Well, she started it," Phoebe said, pointing a finger in C. K.'s direction. "She brought up the *Exorcist*. I don't care if her head does turn around three hundred and sixty-five degrees, but I'm going on record right here and now as being opposed to projectile vomiting. That's way too gross, and besides, I'll bet that green stuff is hell to get out of the carpet."

"I have no intention of vomiting," C. K. said, playing along.

"Bet that's what Linda Blair said," Phoebe answered.

They all giggled. Phoebe had managed to break the tension that engulfed them all. They broke out into full-fledged laughter as they each tried to imitate Linda Blair.

Phoebe glanced up at Piper, standing in the center of the living room. "We needed that. Not that I'm not worried about Leo and Cole."

"And the rest of the world," Piper added. "But you're right. I think we can focus better now."

"So," Paige said. "What now?"

Without warning, Phoebe felt C. K.'s shoulders jerk, then stiffen beneath her arm.

"C. K.?" she asked. "Are you all right?"

In the space of an instant, C. K.'s face had grown pinched and tight, as if she were in pain. Her eyes were enormous. One hand reached out blindly.

"Piper?" she said.

"Right here, sweetie," Piper answered. Swiftly, she moved forward to kneel in front of C. K. and take her hand. Phoebe watched Piper wince at the tightness of the other girl's grip.

"You know that head-turning thing?" C. K. asked. "Get ready. I have a feeling I'm about to really do it . . . *witch!*"

"Whoa," Paige said. "Guess the waiting's over."

"How much longer?" Cole asked. "And I seriously advise you not to use that when-the-time-is-right thing again. I hear that one more time and I won't be held responsible for my actions."

"I don't know what else to tell you," Mileager

De Vermis said. "I'm sorry, but that's the simple truth. There's no way around it. I know this is difficult for you."

"It's difficult for all of us," Leo said.

Cole opened his mouth, then shut it with a snap.

"Sorry, Leo," he said. "I know you're worried, too." He turned to Mileager. "And I know we'll get our chance. I just wish there was something we could do *now*."

"Would it help to see what's going on?" Mileager asked.

"You mean we can?" Cole said.

"Certainly," Mileager said. Before Cole could comment any further, Mileager moved to one of the tapestries which adorned the haven's walls. Cole hadn't paid much attention to it before. But now he noticed it was filled with figures. Their outlines were blurry, difficult to make out.

As he watched, Mileager De Vermis drew in a deep breath, then, murmuring something beneath his breath, he placed his hands upon the tapestry, palms flat. The tapestry rippled slightly, as if a breeze were passing through it. The figures within it snapped sharply into focus.

"That's the living room at Halliwell Manor!" Cole exclaimed. He surged forward, Leo right behind him.

"Don't touch the tapestry!" Mileager warned,

stepping back at exactly the same moment. "Watch!"

Beneath Cole's startled gaze, the figures on the tapestry began to move. It was sort of like watching the world's largest big-screen TV, only made out of cloth.

"There's Phoebe," Cole said.

Leo nodded. "And Piper. Paige and C. K. are with them. They're all together. Things seem to be all right."

For now, Cole thought, resisting the impulse to speak his thought aloud. He had to figure he didn't actually need to do that. Leo knew the score as well as he did, himself.

"Do we know what time it is there?" Cole asked Mileager. "I've sort of lost track of how long we've been here. How much time has gone by?"

"I think I can see the clock on the mantle," Leo said, before Mileager De Vermis could reply. "It's . . ." His normally serious face grew pale. "It's eleven forty-five."

"Fifteen minutes to midnight," Cole said. "This is going to be close."

"Look—look at C. K.!" Leo said, suddenly pointing.

Within the framework of the tapestry, C. K. suddenly pitched forward. She clutched her head, as if in pain, then straightened up abruptly. Even made of thread, not flesh and blood, Cole could see the change come over her. Her face looked pinched and tight. Her eyes, enormous. She reached out with one hand. Swiftly, Piper moved to offer support and comfort.

Then, as Cole watched, C. K.'s features began to blur, as if someone else's were being superimposed over them. Now she was C. K., yet not C. K. C. K. and something, *someone*, more. Beside him, Cole heard Mileager suck in a breath.

"Malvolio!"

Piper tumbled backward as C. K. leaped to her feet without warning. Swiftly, C. K. moved to the center of the living room, putting distance between herself and the Charmed Ones.

"Her face," Phoebe whispered urgently. "Look at her face. I don't think that happened last time. Malvolio's possession of her must be almost total."

Piper nodded as Paige helped her to her feet. "No two ways about it. He's definitely getting stronger."

C. K. looked around the room, her eyes glittering wildly.

"I require a vehicle," she said. "You will provide one."

"Okay," Phoebe said, as she got carefully to her feet. "No problem. Mind if we come along for the ride?"

C. K. smiled. "Foolish witches," she said. "You think that you can stop me? I am stronger than you can possibly imagine. No power on this earth can prevent what I am about to unleash."

"I'll take that as a yes," Phoebe said. She headed for the front hall. Yanking her keys from her purse, she lobbed them across the room toward C. K. "You drive."

Twenty-five

Piper clung to the armrest in the back seat as the Halliwell SUV squealed around a corner. Phoebe rode shotgun, and Paige looked a little pale as she slid around the back with Piper. Piper'd wanted to sit up front beside C. K. herself, but, at the last minute, Phoebe had scooped her.

The SUV took another corner, then revved up a hill. C. K. had been driving with the determination of a predator hot on the scent of its prey for a full ten minutes now. The digital clock display on the dash read 11:55 p.m. Just five minutes left before the potential end of the world.

Unspoken but on all the Charmed Ones' minds were the missing Leo and Cole.

Anything that had the ability to sap the Charmed Ones' concentration had to be considered a weakness. The adversary they were fighting was obviously strong and determined. He'd waited almost five hundred years to accomplish his goal. Much as they worried about Leo and Cole, they knew they simply couldn't afford to do it. Piper leaned forward.

"Have you figured out which portal we're heading to?" she whispered to Phoebe.

But it was Paige who answered, before Phoebe could respond. The SUV took one final, swooping curve up hill, then slowed before a pair of tall wrought iron gates.

"You have got to be kidding me," Paige exclaimed.

They were at a graveyard.

"A graveyard," Leo said. "Well, it does make sense."

"That's some warped sense of humor your brother's got, Mileager," Cole remarked. "Any of the portals would have done the trick. He has to go and pick the one that's in a graveyard."

"Now what?" Leo asked.

"We do what we've been doing," Mileager replied. "Difficult as it is, we watch and wait."

"Don't say it. Let me," Cole put in. "Until the time is right."

Without bothering to switch off the engine, C. K. slid from the driver's side of the SUV and ran toward the cemetery gates.

"Go!" Phoebe cried to Paige and Piper as she leaned across to snatch the keys. The SUV gave a jerk as the engine cut out. "We can't afford to lose her! I'm right behind you."

Piper and Paige scrambled from the car and dashed after C. K. The gates to the cemetery were closed and locked up tight. They were also held in place by a sturdy chain and padlock. It was pretty plain no one was supposed to be admitted after dark.

It took C. K. all of about a minute to open them.

Reaching out, she placed both hands on the gate, one on either side of the padlock. Then she began to murmur an incantation in a language Piper didn't understand, but thought she recognized.

Latin, she thought.

Abruptly, the strange, hot scent of ozone filled Piper's nostrils. She could feel the air almost literally crackle with static electricity. The wind picked up. The places where C. K.'s hands grasped the metal began to glow red, then white.

"Omigod," she heard Phoebe murmur.

White, Piper thought. *White hot.*

With a great cry, C. K. threw back her head and pushed against the gates. Once. Twice. Three times. Cords stood out in her neck with the effort she was making. The wind howled through the trees as if urging her on.

With a shriek of protest, the gates burst open.

Before Piper could so much as take a breath, C. K. was through them, off and running. Her hair waved wildly about her head. Her hands, still glowing white hot, were held straight out in front of her.

"Let's go!" Paige shouted over the wind as she and Phoebe began to race after C. K. "Don't just stand there, Piper! Come on!"

I'm not just standing here, Piper thought a little desperately, as she forced her body into rapid motion. *I'm praying.*

Praying that her brainstorm about how to stop Malvolio De Vermis was right. Because if it wasn't, she was beginning to fear there wasn't a power on earth that could stop what was about to happen.

Not even the Charmed Ones.

Twenty-six

C. K. sped across the graveyard with Phoebe, Paige, and Piper close behind. She seemed to know precisely where she was going. Not once did her footsteps falter.

Phoebe thought she'd remember that journey for the rest of her life. It was a clear, crisp autumn night. November first. For once, no fog had rolled in to obscure either ground or sky. For a place that should be silent, this one seemed alive and full of sounds.

Trees tossed, moaning in the wind. The branches of shrubs rubbed against one another with a sound that set Phoebe's teeth on edge, like fingernails pulled along a blackboard. Even the short cropped grass seemed to have a voice of its own. As the wind passed through it, it made a high-pitched keening sound.

Lights dotted the empty roadways. Here and there, they illuminated a mausoleum or highly-decorated gravestone. Up ahead and to the right, two bright pin spots shone upward onto the face of a stone angel.

That's it, Phoebe realized suddenly, as C. K. abruptly veered toward it. *That's where she's going.*

Malvolio De Vermis was going to bring about the end of the world by melting an angel. Phoebe had to admit, it seemed appropriate. Behind her, in the dark, she heard the clock in the graveyard's chapel begin to sound the hour.

"Do you hear that?" Paige gasped out. "It's midnight."

All Souls' Day was about to begin. Showtime.

C. K. skidded to a stop before the angel, with her hands, still glowing white, held straight out in front of her. As Phoebe watched in horror, the white-hot glow began to spread up C. K.'s arms.

"Paige! Piper!" Phoebe called over the scream of the wind. "We've got to do something!"

"I think I have an idea," Piper called back. "Get over here by me. Add your power to mine."

Phoebe and Paige did as Piper requested, moving quickly to her side. They each put a hand on her shoulder to help channel their energies.

Phoebe could see that the white-hot glow had all but encompassed C. K. now. Above her, she could hear the graveyard clock reach the end of its countdown.

Nine. Ten. Eleven.

A bolt of white-hot light shot from C. K.'s fingertips straight toward the angel, just as Piper raised her own arms.

"Okay, here goes," she shouted. She gave the quick forward motion which meant she was using her own power.

The power to stop time.

For a moment, it seemed to work. The world around the Charmed Ones fell silent as the wind died down. The energy shooting from C. K. halted in its course, just inches from the angel's nose.

"Now what do we do?" Paige panted. "Keep this up for twenty four hours until All Souls' Day is over? Is that even possible?"

"I'm not sure," Piper admitted. "This was the best I could think of on short notice."

"Wait a minute. Something's happening," Phoebe said.

C. K.'s body jerked like a rag doll's, only in slow motion. The energy beam projecting from her fingers flowed forward.

"Wait a minute," Paige said, echoing Phoebe unconsciously. "She's not supposed to be able to do that, is she? She's supposed to stay frozen."

All of a sudden, Phoebe got it. "*She* is frozen," she said. "C. K. is fully here, in our time. But Malvolio De Vermis isn't. In fact, you could say he's outside of time. He's been outside it for five hundred years, trapped in the *De Vermis*

Mysteriis. That's why he can fight Piper's power."

Again C. K.'s body spasmed. Again the energy inched forward. One more motion, and it would reach its destination.

"I really hate to say this," Piper said, her face tight with strain. "But he's winning, you guys. I don't think I can keep this up much longer, even with your help."

As if her words had been all the encouragement Malvolio De Vermis needed, time resumed its regular motion with an audible sound: The sizzle of Malvolio's evil energy connecting with the stone angel.

Piper dropped to her knees, spent.

"I'm sorry," she gasped. "I couldn't hold on."

"It's all right, Piper," Paige consoled, as she knelt down beside her. "You did more than anyone else could."

In front of her, the stone angel now glowed with the same eerie whiteness as Malvolio's evil energy flow. As Phoebe watched, the angel's placid features began to run together as the stone from which it was carved literally began to melt. Then the very air around her seemed to compress.

"Get down flat!" Phoebe shouted as she cast herself face down on the ground.

With a great burst of heat, the angel exploded. Molten rock flew in all directions. There was a great roar, like thunder and waves crashing all combined, followed by a moment of complete and utter silence. The entire world seemed to hold its breath. Then Phoebe felt the ground beneath her begin to shake as a great surge of energy passed over her. The air was filled with a sound she'd never heard before. One she couldn't even begin to describe or identify.

Phoebe lifted up her head.

The dead were all around her.

"The portal's been destroyed," Leo said, his tone urgent, filled with dismay. "The Ward has failed. The energy barrier between the living and the dead has been disrupted."

Cole tore his eyes from the images swirling across the tapestry to focus on Mileager De Vermis. "Things are looking pretty bleak where we come from. Just how much longer do you expect us to stand around and do nothing?"

"We're not doing nothing," Mileager countered, his eyes still fixed on the tapestry. "We're waiting. We're keeping ourselves informed. The time will come, very soon now."

"*How soon?*" Leo asked. "What, exactly, are we waiting for?"

"For my brother," Mileager De Vermis said simply. "He must regain his true form. I cannot leave my haven, my prison, until he leaves his. I have waited for this moment for five hundred years. I think the two of you can wait a little longer."

• • •

"Look at them. They're so happy," Phoebe cried. Head thrown back, she gazed upward. The sky was filled with the spirits of the dead, happily returning to their loved ones on the living side. Like the living they were here to visit, they had no inkling that anything was wrong.

Not yet. But Phoebe had a feeling they would find out, very soon now. Then the images from her vision would start to come true. The dead would turn on the living and begin to destroy them.

"C. K. Where's C. K.?" Paige asked.

"There!" Piper said. Crumpled at the foot of what had once been the angel was a still and silent form. Piper began to crawl toward her, Paige and Phoebe both at her side.

"Do you think she's dead?" Paige asked, her tone urgent. "She can't be dead, I can't heal her if she's dead."

"I don't know," Piper answered. "I hope not. Maybe if she—"

"Piper. Paige. Stop!" Phoebe ordered abruptly.

Piper stared forward. "Omigod."

Something was rising from C. K.'s prone form. It looked like a column of thick, white mist. It rose up, hovering in the air like one of the spirits. Then, still upright, it settled to the ground and began to take on a distinct human form.

"Please tell me that's not who I think it is," Paige said.

No sooner had she finished speaking than a laugh rang out into the night as the figure became completely real. Completely solid. It stretched its arms above its head, as if awakening from a long nap.

"Malvolio De Vermis," Phoebe said.

"At your service, ladies," he said with a smile.

"Okay, there he is! There's your brother!" Cole exclaimed. "That's it. Can we go now?"

"Patience," Mileager De Vermis said.

"*Patience!*" Cole exploded. "Are you nuts? You said you were waiting for your brother, and now he's here. I mean, there. What the hell else are we waiting for?"

"Keep it together, Cole," Leo said suddenly. He laid a hand on Cole's arm. "Watch the tapestry. I think I know."

Twenty-seven

"So, I suppose you think you've won," Piper said as she got to her feet, Paige and Phoebe alongside her.

Malvolio De Vermis laughed again. "Haven't I? I notice you didn't manage to stop me. Your efforts were pretty puny, as a matter of fact."

Piper put her hands on her hips. "Of course you would think so. But then ego never was a problem for you, was it?"

I've got to keep him talking, she thought. She watched as Malvolio moved away from C. K. as if testing out his muscles and enjoying the fact that he could walk once more. He didn't exactly stagger, but his movements were uneven and jerky as if he hadn't quite gotten used to his own physical form.

Gotcha, Piper thought as the last piece of her combined brainstorm/hunch solidified into an actual plan in her mind. It was incredibly risky, to herself most of all. But it was the only way she could think of to bring all the necessary elements together.

Not once did Malvolio glance in C. K.'s direction, she noted. Now that the young woman had served her purpose, Malvolio De Vermis wasn't interested in her anymore.

Fine by me, Piper thought. The less attention Malvolio paid to C. K. the better, as far as Piper was concerned. She slapped a palm to her forehead, exactly as if she'd forgotten something important.

"Wait a minute. What am I talking about?" she went on. "If ego *hadn't* been a problem, you'd have gotten over those issues of brotherly jealousy a long time ago. Say, about five hundred years? Not that I blame you, you understand. It's tough coming in second. Believe me, I should know."

"Piper," Paige whispered as Malvolio De Vermis's face began to darken with rage. Sparks rose from his head as if he was giving off his own electrical charge. His movements became even more jerky as if the energy of his anger was having a negative impact on his ability to adjust to having physical form.

"Please tell me you know what you're doing."

"Believe me," Piper whispered back, "I sincerely hope so."

"Because I think you're really starting to piss him off."

"Good," Piper said.

"What do you mean, good?" Phoebe hissed. "This is the guy who just destroyed a Ward."

"Just get ready to get to C. K., will you guys?" Piper said, putting an end to the discussion. "Get her on her feet and as far away from him as possible. Then remember what the Book of Shadows showed us."

"When?" Phoebe asked.

"This afternoon," Piper said, her tone impatient.

"No, I mean when do we go for C. K.?"

"Don't worry," Piper said. "You'll know."

She stepped away from her sisters toward Malvolio De Vermis.

"And then there's the fact that your brother stuck you inside that book," she continued, raising her voice up a notch. "I mean, let's face it. He won. You lost. That had to hurt in more ways than one. I really hope you're not claustrophobic."

From the corner of her eye, Piper saw C. K. stir, then sit up. Phoebe and Paige began to slowly move toward her.

Malvolio De Vermis gave a snarl. "You try my patience, witch," he cried. "Do not tempt my rage, I warn you."

"Oh, for crying out loud," Piper exclaimed as she took another step toward him. "Do you have to sound so hokey? You're definitely going to want to brush up on your language skills, particularly those threats. 'Do not tempt my rage' went out about two hundred years ago."

With a roar of rage, Malvolio De Vermis raised his arms and hurled a stream of angry red energy straight at Piper.

Paige and Phoebe dashed to C. K. and helped her to her feet, urging her away from Malvolio. At the very last moment, Piper threw herself to one side. The energy stream struck a headstone. It disappeared in a ball of fire. Piper let the momentum carry her into a roll, then to her feet, just the way Phoebe had taught her.

"Gee," she said as she turned back to Malvolio. "You missed me. Guess maybe you're a little rusty."

Again, Malvolio raised his arms above his head.

"No!" C. K. suddenly cried out. "Piper!"

Malvolio De Vermis hurled a second wave of energy. With a flick of her fingers, Piper froze it. It hung in the air like a giant ring of fire.

"Hey, look, now it works," she said. Feigning casualness, she stepped to one side, then unfroze the energy stream. It struck a stand of shrubs that, just moments ago, had been behind her. At once, the plants burst into flames.

"Congratulations," Piper said. "You've just proved you can start a campfire."

The very air around Malvolio De Vermis

seemed to seethe with rage. "I will be damned," he said through clenched teeth. "Before I let a woman outsmart me."

"Don't take it so personally," Piper advised, her tone deliberately condescending. "I outsmart puny little mages like you every day."

Malvolio De Vermis gave an outraged bellow. "You think you're so smart," he said. "But no witch is smarter than I am!" He raised his hands above his head. "Dead ones, hear me!" he cried. "Hear what this witch has done this night. You have come to visit your loved ones as you always do. But this witch has *destroyed your ability to go back*."

Piper resisted the impulse to sneak a glance in her sisters' direction. Malvolio De Vermis seemed to have forgotten the others completely. All his energy was focused on Piper. She'd worked hard to achieve exactly that. Now was no time to blow it.

"I have an exceptionally bad feeling about this," Paige whispered.

"You and me both," Phoebe answered.

The spirits of the dead began to gather around Malvolio. They floated in the air above his head. Moving in ever-tightening circles, like a whirlwind in the making, their attention fixed on Piper.

"You cannot return to the place where you belong," Malvolio continued. "You must stay in the world of the living forever. But you will never be alive. *You will always be dead.* Your loved ones will come to fear and hate you. They will turn on you and drive you away. You will be outcasts in the world of the living, forever."

At Malvolio's words, the spirits of the dead began to wail. The sound was high-pitched, agonized. Piper felt it sear right through her head.

"All this, the witch has done," Malvolio De Vermis shouted. "Do not let her go unpunished. As you will suffer, let her suffer also. *Take your revenge!*"

"Piper! No!" C. K. shouted.

But her call was drowned out by the cries of the dead. Their wailing increased in pitch and intensity. Then, as if spiraling around Malvolio had wound them into a vortex too tight to hold, the dead exploded outward, heading straight for Piper.

A young child reached her first, swooping around behind her and clinging to her back. It fisted its hands in Piper's hair. Piper cried out in pain as it yanked her head back.

"Phoebe, it's your vision. It's coming true," Paige whispered in dismay.

"I know," Phoebe said.

"No, oh no," C. K. moaned. She clung to Paige and Phoebe as all three watched in mounting horror. Piper made no move to fend off the spirits. "Why doesn't she fight back? Why don't you help her?"

"Because you're the only one who can do

that, C. K.," Phoebe answered steadily.

"What do you mean? I don't know what you mean!" C. K. said. Desperately, she began to struggle against Paige and Phoebe's hold. "Let go of me! Let me go to Piper."

"You don't need to go to Piper," Paige said. "You can save her from right here."

"How?" C. K. demanded wildly as Piper cried out in pain again. "Tell me how!"

"Be part of the solution, just the way Piper wanted you to."

All of a sudden, C. K. stopped struggling. "My grief," she said. "You want me to accept what they're feeling," she gestured to the spirits clustered around Piper. "Outrage. Grief. Pain."

"It doesn't matter what we want. It's what *you* want, C. K.," Phoebe said. "You couldn't help Jace. You *can* help Piper. But only if it's what you truly want."

"It is," C. K. said.

As if her words had been a summons, the shadow which had attacked Piper at Halliwell Manor burst into being, so dark and dense it blotted out the stars above their heads.

"Let go of me, please," C. K. instructed.

Phoebe and Paige did as she asked. Releasing her arms, they stepped back. C. K. lifted her hands above her head.

At her gesture, Malvolio De Vermis seemed to remember their presence. He turned toward them.

"No!" he yelled.

"Too late," Phoebe said.

"You are mine. Come back to me," C. K. called out. She spread her arms open wide. At once the shadow streaked toward her, striking her in the center of her chest—the very center of her broken heart.

The force of the impact knocked C. K. off her feet. She flew backward through the air, then hit the grass with a *thud*. Paige and Phoebe dashed to her side.

C. K. lay flat on her back. Her eyes were open wide, unblinking. Her hands were pressed against her unmoving chest. Then, as Paige and Phoebe watched, C. K. blinked and pulled in one long, ragged breath.

"Look," Phoebe said.

Tears streamed down C. K. Piers's cheeks.

"She's done it," Paige said.

Twenty-eight

"At last!" Mileager De Vermis cried. "At long last, the time is right!"

"Finally!" Cole barked.

Mileager turned from the tapestry to face Leo and Cole. "Thank you for coming here," he said. "Now, I will end what was begun so long ago. I will do whatever must be done. I do not think that we will meet again."

"Good luck," Leo said.

"And to you," Mileager said with a faint smile. "I'd be ready to leave by whatever means you came," he warned. "Now that this haven no longer has a reason to exist, it won't last for very much longer."

As if his words had been a signal, the room in which they were standing began to tremble, then to rock. The walls began to dissolve. Leo staggered as the floor beneath his feet abruptly gave way. Cole grabbed him by the arm.

"Let's get out of here," he said.

"Right with you," Leo agreed.

"I certainly hope so," Cole replied.

Leo grasped Cole by the shoulder and began to orb. The last thing he saw was the haven dissolving around him as Mileager De Vermis vanished in a flash of searing white light.

"Piper! I'm coming!" Paige called.

While Phoebe stayed with C. K., Paige raced toward where Piper lay huddled on the ground. Her face was bloody and scratched. Her clothing was torn. But at least the spirits had stopped their deadly attack. They milled agitatedly in the air around her like an uncertain crowd.

C. K.'s decision to accept her own grief was plainly having an effect, helping to counterbalance Malvolio's evil powers. Now all the Charmed Ones needed was one thing to tip the scales completely in their favor.

"Are you all right?" Paige gasped as she dropped to Piper's side. She helped her to sit up.

"Don't worry about me," Piper said. "I'll be fine. How's C. K. doing?"

"Crying."

"That's great," Piper said. "Has the cavalry showed?"

"Not yet," Paige said. "But I'm hoping they'll be here any minute now."

"Look!" Phoebe suddenly cried. Between

where the sisters crouched, the air began to shimmer bright blue. Leo and Cole orbed into view.

"Oh, thank goodness!" Piper sobbed.

Instantly, the pair split up. Leo ran to Piper's side, and Cole to Phoebe's.

"Get ready," he said. "I think we're about to have the big finale."

No sooner had he finished speaking than Mileager De Vermis burst into view opposite his brother. For a moment, the two twins stood, staring at one another. It was their first meeting in five hundred years.

"So," Malvolio De Vermis said. "It will end here."

"It will," Mileager confirmed. "One way or the other."

"I decide how it will end!" Malvolio screamed in fury. "All my life, you have come first. Now, you can be the first to die!"

He raised his arms and shot a stream of pure, dark energy straight at his brother. Mileager made no attempt to avoid it. Instead, he stepped forward!

"What on earth is he doing?" Paige asked.

"What he has to," Leo answered solemnly.

The pulse of energy struck Mileager full in the chest. He staggered backward a few steps, then kept on coming.

"Fight! Why won't you fight?" Malvolio cried. He launched another wave of energy. Again,

Mileager did nothing to avoid it. The second pulse of energy brought him to his knees.

He got to his feet, and kept on coming.

"I will not fight you, Malvolio," he said. He took another step toward him. "I will not fight myself. We are the same, you and I."

"That isn't true!" Malvolio De Vermis panted. "I'm nothing like you! Nothing!"

Mileager took another step, then another. Only a few footsteps separated them now. "Oh, yes you are," he said. "And I am like you. Together, we were formed. Together, we will die. That is the only way for us. Neither can exist without the other. Haven't you figured that out yet?"

He opened his arms as if offering an embrace.

Malvolio De Vermis's face was a mass of twisted emotions. Hope tangled with hate. Pain with love.

"No!" he cried. "I tell you, no! I have hated you all my life. I won't stop now."

"You haven't hated me, Malvolio," Mileager said. He took the remaining steps to stand directly before his brother. "You never hated me. You hated yourself."

With a great cry, Malvolio dropped to his knees, his face in his hands. Without hesitation, Mileager dropped down beside him. He placed one arm upon his brother's shoulder. Malvolio's body gave a jerk, and then was still.

"Let us put an end to hate, an end to strife. Give me your hand, Malvolio."

Malvolio De Vermis lifted his head. For a moment, the two brothers stared at one another. Then, slowly, Malvolio raised one arm and placed his hand upon Mileager's shoulder. It was the mirror image of the way Mileager clasped him. For the first time in five hundred years, the brothers were joined together.

"So," Malvolio said.

Mileager De Vermis smiled. "Well done, brother. At last, it is over."

As his words ended, the brothers were engulfed in a hot, white light. Paige lifted a hand to cover her eyes. When she lowered it again, the brothers had vanished. For a moment, their outline seemed to hang in the air. Thin, white lines lay superimposed on the darkness. Then even these slowly faded from view.

"Mileager was right," she said. "It *is* over."

"Not quite," Phoebe said as she and Cole joined the others. "Look!" She pointed.

C. K. stood where Phoebe and Cole had left her. But she wasn't alone. A spirit hovered at her side. C. K.'s face was radiant as she faced the ghost.

"Jace," Paige said. "He's come back!"

"My guess is he was here all along," Piper said softly. "But she couldn't see him until she accepted the fact that he was gone."

"I suppose that makes sense," Phoebe

acknowledged. "In a reverse-psychology sort of way." She looked at Piper's torn clothes and scratched face. "Are you all right?"

"I could go for a nice hot bath and a round with the first aid kit," Piper acknowledged. "But, yeah, basically, I'm all right."

"What you did was one of the bravest things I've ever seen," Cole said. "Though I don't think Leo appreciated it very much."

"It scared me to death," Leo said. "Metaphorically speaking, of course." He gave Piper's shoulders a squeeze. "But it also made me proud of her."

"Let's go home," Paige proposed, her voice wry. "All this couples mushiness is starting to make me nauseous."

Twenty-nine

In spite of her exhausting night, Piper was up early the next morning. She puttered alone in the kitchen enjoying the sun streaming through the windows, the scent of brewing coffee. A sense of well-being seemed to permeate the air.

Things are back in balance, Piper thought as she mixed flour, sugar, salt, and baking powder together in her favorite blue mixing bowl. She cut in butter, then added the liquid ingredients she'd prepared earlier. She poured it into a pan, then dribbled streusel mixture on top. A moment later, she was sliding a batch of Gram's famous coffee cake into the oven.

C. K. had accepted her fiancé's death. The De Vermis brothers had accepted each other. Their reconciliation had healed the energy barrier between the living and the dead. At midnight tonight, All Souls' Day would be over. The dead would return to their own realm for another year.

About as normal as it gets around here, Piper thought as she set the oven timer. She wasn't foolish enough to think there would never be another crisis, but she was grateful for a job well done.

"Hey, what are you doing up so early?" Phoebe's voice asked. "And what have you done with the coffee?"

"It's right where it always is," Piper answered. She poured Phoebe a cup. "What?"

"You made coffee cake, didn't you?" Phoebe asked. "Prue's favorite."

Piper nodded. "Uh huh. I guess it was because I woke up thinking about her. Do you think her spirit ever comes back, Phoebes?"

Phoebe considered for a moment. "I honestly don't know, Piper. But wherever she is, I know Prue loves us, just like we love her. That's something that will never change."

"I know," Piper said softly.

"You think C. K. will be okay?" Phoebe asked after a moment. She took the coffee from Piper and leaned against the kitchen counter.

"Yes," Piper answered as she began to wash her mixing bowls. "I think so. Though I do think she'll need some help discovering the full extent of her powers. I was thinking maybe Paige could take that on."

"Paige could take what on?" Paige asked from the doorway. "Why aren't you two still in bed? Are you abnormal or something?"

"We could ask you the same question," Phoebe said with a laugh.

"Absolutely not," Paige said. "No more questions until I've had some coffee." She poured herself a cup, then settled in beside Phoebe. "So, what's my assignment?"

"I was thinking you might mentor C. K.," Piper said as she turned off the water and dried her hands on a nearby towel. "You know, sort of show her the magic ropes. She's got a lot of catching up to do."

"I know what that feels like," Paige acknowledged. "Sure, I'll be happy to help. She's coming over tomorrow morning, right?"

"Right," Phoebe nodded. "I wasn't entirely happy about leaving her on her own, but it seemed only right to give her and Jace as much time together as possible."

"Speaking of guys, where are the ones who always seem to hang around here?" Paige inquired.

Piper rolled her eyes. "Believe it or not, the Elders summoned Leo at the crack of dawn. I hope they're not being too hard on him," she said as she stole a quick glance at the coffee cake. It was just beginning to rise. The scent of warm butter and sugar began to fill the kitchen.

"Cole went for a run," Phoebe said. "After checking under the passenger seat of the SUV one more time. I think he's half convinced the *De Vermis Mysteriis* is going to turn up again."

On the way back to Halliwell Manor the previous night, Cole had discovered that the book was gone. Leo thought it had vanished with the De Vermis brothers. Cole remained unconvinced. The discussion had finally been settled by Paige who had accurately remarked that only time would tell.

"Coffee cake," Paige said suddenly. "That's what I smell."

Piper turned to her with a smile. "You're just now figuring that out?"

"Give me a break," Paige said. "My sense of smell is just waking up. I love your coffee cake, Piper. It's my favorite."

"Actually, it's Grams's recipe. And it was Prue's favorite, too," Piper said after a moment.

"Oh," Paige said. "Okay. I can deal with that. Liking something Prue liked is kind of a good feeling. It makes me feel connected to her, somehow."

"You are connected to her," Phoebe said simply. "We all are. Just like we're connected to one another. That's what makes us the Charmed Ones."

"Does this mean I can have the biggest piece?" Paige asked.

Delighted, Piper laughed. "That's exactly what Prue used to ask," she said. "I'll tell you the same thing I always told her."

"Yes, of course," Paige suggested helpfully.

"You can set the table," Piper said.

Paige gave a mock groan.

"I'll help," Phoebe offered. She put an arm around Paige's shoulders as, eyes laughing, they both looked expectantly at Piper.

"All right, I'll help too. It's not like I can't take a hint," Piper exclaimed.

"Good dishes?" Paige asked.

"The best," Piper concurred.

Together, the Charmed Ones performed the simple task, happy to be in the bright sunshine of a brand-new day.